Sheltered Lives

When H. and I were younger we expected life after we left home to be like a Katherine Mansfield story—blue bowls reflected in polished table tops, all color and texture and sensitivity, and no loud voices. Both of us became careful housekeepers because we thought that by arranging our surroundings, we could control them. Untrue.

"An admirer of Jane Austen, she [Mary Hazzard] probes the ironies of truths concealed beneath the surfaces of things, misunderstandings between men and women, the apparent conflict between the realistic and romantic views of life."

—*Library Journal*

Sheltered Lives

by Mary Hazzard

PINNACLE BOOKS NEW YORK

This is a work of fiction. All the characters and events portrayed in this book are fictional, and any resemblance to real people or incidents is purely coincidental.

SHELTERED LIVES

A Pinnacle Books edition, published by special arrangement with Madrona Publishers, Inc.

First printing, August, 1981

ISBN: 0-523-41430-7

Cover illustration by Marie Fay

Printed in the United States of America

PINNACLE BOOKS, INC.
1430 Broadway
New York, New York 10018

Sheltered Lives

"Lies are all very well in their place but the truth seems to me so much more interesting . . ."

—Frieda Lawrence, *"Not I, but the Wind"*

"Seldom, very seldom does complete truth belong to any human disclosure, seldom can it happen that something is not a little disguised, or a little mistaken."

—Jane Austen, *Emma*

1

May, 18, 1969

Dear Nat—

I'm sorry about the telephone receiver in the Kleenex box. A woman called to sell me upholstery or something, and when the phone rang and it wasn't you, I was so angry that I punished her by setting the receiver down softly and sneaking away. You must have wondered.

You had said you would call before noon, and it was three by then. But you wouldn't have been able to come with me that day anyway, would you? You did ask me to wait, and I apologize for not waiting.

I meant to write a cheerful note explaining about the telephone, and I have begun to complain already.

I love you.

Anne

May 16—Penn.

Deer Crossing 2 Mi.

" " 1-1/2 Mi.

" " 1 Mi.

(No deer)

A Clean Car Has Class

Budget Beauty Salon

(Hills packed with rows of rusting abandoned cars.)
Register Communists, not Guns!
Support Your Right to Bear Arms.
(This in a Texaco station I had gone to because of the opera. I saw the notice posted inside when I went to get the key to the ladies' room. Four men sitting in a semicircle next to it. Red, tough faces and hostile expressions as if they had put their sign up two minutes before, just to get my reaction. Yet it was faded, must have been there long enough for them to have stopped seeing it. Must I boycott Texaco now?)
(Magic Fingers in bed in motel, 25¢. Disappointing. A weak, trapped motor in the mattress. Like having a wind-up toy under your pillow. You keep waiting for it to run down, are relieved when it does.)

May 17—Harrisonburg, Va.
Pistols Bought and Sold
No Waiting Period
Freezer Cooler
We Freeze to Please
The Sinner (sign on old black car)
(Winchester, Va. Pretty town—roses, stone and brick houses on street. Movie double bill. Twisted Sex & 50,000 B.C. (before clothes).)
(Big ribbed aluminum trucks, saying TIME or P.I.E.)
Grimm Realty Co.
In This Town
We Believe in Freedom
(red, white, & blue, with stars)
Hungry Mother State Park
(What is wrong with me? I have wanted to see Monticello all my life, and yet I sped past the exit to Charlottesville as if I lived in the next town and could go there any time I wanted. Why take this route if I'm not going to see anything but road signs and motel rooms?)

May 18—Tenn.

1/4 Mi. Fudge's Chapel, Methodist
Sinking creek
Count your Blessings, then your mistakes.
COUPLE 6$ Interstate Motel
Pray to be Stronger, Not for an Easy Life.
(This flood of moral advice seems to be regional. Not being used to it, I can't help taking it personally and wanting to argue. Signs in the Northeast don't tell you to do much more than yield or squeeze right or buy something.)
Stop Pests in your House.
Chew Furniture
(Not unless I get desperate. Stop. Place try to realize that there are people named Chew. Charles Chew. Louise Chew.)
Old Plantation BarBQ
"Yas Suh! It's Cooked in De Pit!" (!)
Shoot Looters
(Bumper Sticker. Red, white, & blue, with stars.)

May 19—Arkansas

Boggy Bayou (tenant cabins by road at edge of field, two front doors on each)
Malvern Skating Rink Enjoying Skating on Plastic
Gross Mortuary
Cold Beer to Go
Arkansas Alligator Farm
"Odd, Strange Curios"
Hot Springs Most Notable Sight
Nunnery's Cleaners
Good Shepherd Laundry
Razorback Stores

May 20—Plateau, Okla.

(turtles on road)
VICE Superette

(Competition between two Reptile Ranches, sixteen mi. apart)
Dont Wait Dont Wait
See the Orion Reptile Ranch
Den of Death
8 Kind of Rattlesnakes
Rare Reptiles from China
Fun for the Entire Family
Underwood's Steak House
Feed Your Hunger Good
(Cemetery next to sign "Worms for Sale")

May 21—Tucumcari, N.M.
(Light on both sides of road. You could drive straight off the edge of the earth.)
(VW bus full of Indians eating ice cream cones)

May 22—Santa Fe

The words on signs don't matter any more. The landscape has taken over. Desert, the first I've seen in real life. Those stiff gray-green bushes everywhere have to be sage, and I concede that there is such a thing as tumbleweed. It comes in frail, clenched bunches that catch in the lower strands of barbed-wire fences. Although I am further above sea level all the time, the land still looks flat except for occasional rock formations that bear a disturbing resemblance to the ruins of abandoned cities. Only the road itself, the asphalt, is really familiar. A few agressive trucks, not many cars.

An unsettling feeling: Two hawks circled over the plain as I approached the town, and I suddenly saw myself from their point of view—a tense profile in heavy sunglasses, just visible in the open window of a tan station wagon climbing through the tan landscape—as if I were taking part in the opening shot of a movie, probably made by a foreign director, about the spiritual emptiness of America. A very cinematic landscape, fit only for movies or dreams.

The town itself is strange too, but inviting. Adobe buildings, mostly pink, white, peach, or tan, surround a plaza where Indians sit on the sidewalk with jewelry spread out for sale on blankets. I rejected all the Mexican food signs and found this Chinese restaurant, exactly like one in Albany. Tea and Egg Foo Yung. Only two o'clock now. If you travel from east to west, with all the zone changes, time spreads out along with space. But I can't stop to see anything here; I am afraid of losing momentum. The top of my head feels empty now, and my hands are almost too heavy to lift. Altitude?

Arroyo Seco

There really is no point in my being sensitive every time H says something extravagant. Why should I require her to be different from other people, just because she is my sister? I mustn't let H irritate me.

I haven't finished describing Santa Fe or the rest of the trip here. Entrance to the S.F. Opera on the far side of the town. Expensive suburb? Adobe houses on bare hills, but these have patios and picture windows. Mountains in distance, purple-green with snow on top.

Los Alamos not far from the highway. Tall green mesa standing in convenient isolation against a background of cliffs and piled clouds. Harmless looking. Like a castle for a princess.

Espanola. "Peachs for sale," "Toematos," signs on

empty roadside stands. Gas station attendant, brown face and straight black hair, filled my car with an unknown brand of gas and carried on a conversation in Spanish with a friend who lounged against a wall. Certainly about the car and possibly about me. He couldn't get over the number of bumper stickers and the McCarthy flower on the rear window, and I don't think he'd seen a Hillman before. (Or heard one; the car growls like a truck on hills. Sounds more powerful as it gets weaker, ever since Arkansas exhaust-pipe trouble that baffles all mechanics. Our Fulbright souvenir is wearing out.)

Green valley with rows of fruit trees. Rio Grande follows the line of the road there. Later it falls to the bottom of a deep gorge, and I could see it only as a curving, narrow canyon on my left. Storm in the distance, while I was still driving through afternoon sunshine on the hill before Taos valley. Clouds blue-black, with lightning, and rain that looked like gray mist. Then something really strange, and so vacantly symbolic that I laughed out loud: The clouds shifted and there was a rainbow, meeting the ground on the other side of the town, in approximately the spot where I had estimated that H's house must be.

There wasn't a sign of the storm when I drove into the yard and saw H standing in the doorway of this low white house. Hollyhocks in front, mountains behind, and one blond daughter on each side of her. "You're here," she called when I got out of the car. She came forward smiling and holding out her arms. "We're roasting a chicken for you, and we've made bread."

I wanted to say something that would live up to the smell of baking coming from the door. "Did you know," I asked Melisande, "that a few minutes ago you were in the middle of a rainbow?"

Melisande sighed. She is twelve now and accurate in spotting grown-up sentimentality. Nora looked serious and pointed to the mountains. "No," she said, "the rainbow was *there*."

"We get them all the time," Melisande said, as if rainbows were cockroaches.

But Harriet still smiled. We got my suitcase out of the car, and she led the way through the fragrant kitchen to a small bedroom with deep window ledges and a tiny curved fireplace in the corner. "We've put you in here since there's only one of you." She paused delicately.

"Nat couldn't . . ." I told her.

"Yes. You said." I was glad I had called her from Tucumcari. "Shall we have some tea?" She flipped back the thick, dark braid that hung over one shoulder and ran into the kitchen to take two brown loaves out of the oven. "There's only one thing more satisfying than having a baby," she said as I followed her in, "and that's baking bread."

That was the remark that got on my nerves so, because it was such a fake wise-woman thing to say. She couldn't have expected me to be impressed, and yet there was nobody else to hear her except the girls.

But I think all I said was, "More satisfying? I wouldn't know."

May 23 (just after midnight)

Carved spiral posts hold up the porch roof. Porch is not a porch but a *portal,* accent on second syllable. The round roof beams *(vigas)* show on the outside.

The Sangre de Cristo mountains, green with purple shadows in diagonal folds. The purple turns almost red at sunset and glows. Cottonwood trees and poplars. Piñon. Irrigation ditches. All the buildings either adobe or plastered cement block. First Methodist Church is pink. Clear, pure air that I think I'll be able to breathe.

H has changed again. Before I came, I kept thinking of the last time I saw her (Nearly seven years ago? It can't be, but it must because it was when she came home for my wedding.), and I almost dreaded meeting her today. I was afraid I would find only a more extreme version of the desperate, childworn young mother she appeared to have become at the time of that visit. I remember how shocked I was by her clothes then—out of date and specked with cookie crumbs and diaper lint—entirely uncharacteristic of her, I thought. I didn't understand that she simply didn't belong in Massachusetts any more. She was so beautiful in the doorway this afternoon, in a striped orange and yellow skirt and a white Mexican blouse trimmed with coarse lace. (I suspect the origin of the skirt; the cloth resembles the pattern of an Indian bedspread Mother sent her once.) Walking into the parsonage in the same clothes, she would probably look like an aging Radcliffe student pretending to be a peasant. Here she is just right, a thin Frieda Lawrence.

I suppose that for the rest of my life I will continue to think of H as my beautiful sister. I don't think I was jealous of her when we were growing up (not for that, anyway), because my mother considered beauty more of a burden than anything else. Besides, if I didn't have H's delicate bones or luminous eyes, how could I be certain I wouldn't someday develop them? It was H's spirit that was the most attractive thing about her, though I don't think Mother knew that. Her intensity. She could concentrate all her energy on whatever she happened to be talking about, and other people had to listen. That was why men liked her so much and why she became an actress.

That same intensity made her difficult to live with sometimes. "Get out of my room," she could scream at me when my father, tired of making conversation with the boy who was waiting for her, sent me upstairs to ask her to hurry. At one period, if H was at home in the afternoon or evening, there was nearly always some young man sitting on the edge of our couch and glancing at the stairway. And although my father would certainly have preferred to be in his study planning next Sunday's sermon, he was conscious of a duty to get acquainted with his daughter's boyfriends, and he tried very hard. After a while, though, I think he began to feel that there were too many of them for him possibly to know, and he gave up. I think, too, that he may have suspected he was confusing them with each other, giving a hearty greeting to a boy he had never seen before or calling him by the wrong name. There was one horrible occasion I remember when a boy named Dud sat there and let himself be called Chuck long after it was too late for correction and I knew what his name was and he knew that I knew it. He looked more tortured every minute, and I don't think he came to our house again; even H wasn't worth that.

Or, in another mood, she might invite me into her room to sit on a corner of the bed that was piled with crinolines and rejected dresses and give my opinion of the hair styles she was experimenting with. She asked for my advice as if what I said would be important, though I don't remember whether she ever took it.

But when H came home seven years ago and we met her at the airport, she had changed. Her two little girls climbed out of the plane first, and H was behind them with the baby looking over her shoulder from a sling on her back. All that showed of eight-month-old Tomas, besides a waving fist, was the impossibly big face that babies seem to have if you're not used to them, all cheeks and forehead. He and the girls were chubby and tanned, and the girls' off-white hair reached their shoulder blades. H's hair was loose too, and her skirt hung four inches below an old camel's-hair coat. She wore Indian moccasins and had a bulging raffia bag slung over one arm.

"There she is," I said when I recognized her smiling haggardly toward the barrier behind which N and I stood. I could hardly believe it was H, and I felt I had to explain. "She's tired," I said. "It was a long trip, and she probably had to hold the baby all the way." I had told N so much about how beautiful she was.

"Of course," he said.

The girls were running toward us in their long, faded skirts, carrying various paper bags and other bundles. Some Japanese tourists next to us nudged each other excitedly and took their picture. "I'd better not kiss you," H said when she reached us. "The baby was sick all over my blouse."

Back home in the parsonage, with the little girls climbing over my father in the study and my mother rocking the baby to sleep upstairs, H regained some of her glamour. Because it was cold for early September, N made hot grog, and H brushed her hair smooth and came down to the living room wearing a blue kimono. We sat by the fireplace with our steaming cups, and H told us about New Mexico and Seth's paintings and her interesting friends and the work she was doing with an amateur theatre group that she hoped to persuade to produce *The Sea Gull* with herself as Nina. Her eyes glowed in the way I had described, and N, in spite of his first impression, began to see that I wasn't entirely deluded on the subject of my sister. Looking at her then, I noticed that she had put on make-up since we got home. I don't know why she had chosen to look as she did on the plane except that she has always thrown herself into any part she happens to be cast in. She may have been deliberately contrasting her appearance with mine, to show N how attractive I was or to signal to me that she wasn't going to try to steal him from me. But perhaps she was, as I had told N, just tired.

I was afraid H might expect us to be more excited about our wedding than we were. She had made such a production of hers that I didn't think she could understand how little the ceremony meant to N and me. It was something to go through with only because not having a traditional wedding would be even more complicated. It wasn't because we didn't care about each other and expect to live together for the rest of our lives; we did. (Yes, we did.) But we both, I think, thought of our marriage as a private agreement between ourselves, and we wished we could keep everyone else out of it. On the other hand, we were realistic enough to see how impossible that would be, and how cruel to our families.

The arrangements had already begun to get out of hand by the time H arrived. The ceremony had been shifted from the small chapel to the sanctuary because of the hundreds of biologists N's mother had to invite if she invited anyone at all, and my mother had talked me into wearing white instead of pale green, although luckily I was five inches too tall for H's Botticelli wedding dress. The organist refused to believe I meant it when I told her to play anything that happened to come into her head, and since I was being forced to make a choice, I had admitted to her (in front of my distressed mother) that I disliked Wagner only a little more than Mendelssohn and would prefer it if she could stick to Bach. Archaic silver and crystal objects had come in the mail, scattering excelsior all over the rugs and taking us somehow by surprise. N and I had suddenly become the appalled owners of a silent butler and a sterling silver tray meant for calling cards, and we were beginning to feel pushed around. If H had jumped into the situation and tried to add some of her personal flourishes to the whole business, I think we would have eloped. As it was, she was too busy to interfere, and the only characteristic touch she added was an extra gift to us of a bottle of imported champagne, which I knew she couldn't afford, and two crystal glasses with spirals of air in their stems. Her formal present was a small painting that Seth had done years ago before he went abstract and that she knew I liked.

It was less than a week before the wedding when H and the children came, and she didn't really talk to me much about Seth or New Mexico or the way she lived. By the end of each day she seemed usually to be exhausted, and when the children were up she spent most of her time feeding them or answering their questions or wandering around with a dirty diaper in one hand. She quarreled a lot with Mother about things like pacifiers and toilet training and baby food. H was in the middle of a health-food phase, and Mother cringed whenever she saw her spooning a mixture of wheat germ, brewers' yeast, ground vitamin pills, and molasses into little Tomas. "But does the poor little thing like it?" Mother asked, a question being the severest type of criticism she usually allows herself. "He loves it," H said, and Tomas, strong as a young tiger, would bat at the spoon and growl for more.

I discovered that I enjoyed being an aunt. I read stories to the little girls and held Tomas when I could, reciting verses from the *Oxford Book of Nursery Rhymes* and bouncing him to make him chuckle. But I couldn't stand (as I had never been able to) the arguments that went on between H and my mother. I would start into the kitchen to offer to help with the feeding, and then I would hear H's voice, raised and defiant: "But it makes you feel wonderful," she would be saying. "It takes away depression, fatigue, anxiety." And she would add meaningly, "It wouldn't hurt you to try it." And I would retreat.

The toilet-training quarrels were partly the ideological ones you might expect between the two generations involved, and I was on H's side except when she got personal. ("Look at her," she commanded, waving her index finger at me as N and I came in together after getting his parents settled at the local inn. "A methodical, neurotic perfectionist. That's what you get with rigid toilet training." My mother, sinking in a mixture of hurt feelings and sympathy for me, couldn't think of anything to say, but N looked at H in wonderment. "And how," he asked her gently, "did they get *you*?") But Mother's main objection was to

H's method of training, which was to let two-year-old Nora go without diapers "so she can see what's happening." What was happening was that little puddles were appearing on the floors and even on the Persian rug. Mother kept following Nora around and trying, when it seemed appropriate, to steer her towards the bathroom. "You're making her feel guilty, Mother," H said. "It's a natural function."

When the children were in bed for their naps, H wandered through the house touching things. Often she sat on the piano bench, playing Chopin fiercely until she had made enough mistakes to see that it was hopeless and then just sitting there looking down at her hands and dripping tears onto the keys. She and Seth couldn't afford a piano, she told me, and anyway they were always moving from one house to another.

H complicated our wedding only by bringing back the feelings I always had when she was there. If I felt overpowered by her, it wasn't her fault, I suppose.

N was having his own family problems. His Episcopalian mother liked me well enough but was nervous about the ceremony because she was convinced that Unitarians could be counted on only to do something weird. The prospect of what her friends might think if somebody happened to chant Hare Krishna or Shalom or anything at all gave her shivers in spite of our reassurances. N's father, an agnostic scientist who avoids all churches and consequently has too much respect for them, had the more realistic fear of having to think of things to talk about with my father during the social occasions preceding the wedding. As it was, they managed by avoiding politics and God (in whom my father has an unfashionable belief) and discussing the effects of DDT. (Father's *Silent Spring* sermon, delivered two weeks later, was one of his greatest successes, Mother wrote, and he repeated it once a year until his retirement.)

As soon as we could, N and I fled from all of them, with our steamer trunk packed with sweaters, wool socks, and copies of *Bleak House* and *Our Mutual Friend* for reading aloud on long winter evenings in a foreign land. The last time I saw H before today she was wearing rose-colored velveteen, standing in front of a window in the parish hall to take advantage of back-lighting, and smiling at one of N's bachelor friends over a cup of rose-colored punch. She was doing her best for me, but she looked more hysterical than radiant.

This is all true, but I see that I must have resented H then even more than I knew. I still think that what I minded most (Why?) was the change in her and the evidence of waste. (Treachery? Was that why? So much of the energy and spirit she had before her marriage had gone into imagining a wonderful future, for me as well as for herself. We were different from ordinary people, she always said. Other people grew old and discouraged only because they didn't see that it wasn't necessary; but we could do anything. I had believed her, and then on that visit I saw her using the same kind of energy only to fuss over her children, as if she hadn't ever had any other plan for her life.)

But that seems to be over now. The children are older, and she doesn't hover over them. (Maybe she didn't then except when away from home, because of not having anything else to do? Or she was using them as a barrier between herself and any questions we might ask about her own life. That production of *The*

Sea Gull never came off, or she would have sent me a program.)

I still don't know why she chose to marry Seth Huggins. Maybe because he's a genius, if he is, which is hard to believe. He's just the same as he was twelve years ago. Square face, reddish-brown hair that matches the rims of his glasses, a scratchy voice, and he's never been slim. This somewhat hostile description of him is, I suppose, my revenge for the way he behaves. He didn't even pretend to be glad to see me after all these years—just came into the kitchen, said "Hi. What's for supper?", washed his hands at the sink, cut a piece of bread for himself, and sat at the table eating the bread and looking grumpy. If H forgot to tell him I was coming, he should at least have been surprised. She explained afterwards that he's preoccupied, working on a problem in his latest painting. I thought artists were supposed to be lively, I told her, flashing their eyes and pouring more wine for everybody. I was referring to something she had said just before her wedding, when she was explaining how different her life would be from those of her friends who had married teachers or data processing experts. But she has grown up. "This isn't *La Bohème,*" she said tonight. "This is life."

May 24

I didn't expect to write in this notebook last night, but I couldn't sleep. Everything in the room looked strange—the Indian blankets, the sheepskin rug, the carved table next to the bed, and especially the swollen papier-mâché doll dangling from a beam above my head. It wore a costume made from strips of blue and white tissue paper, and there was a black shape on its chest that worried me because I suspected a spider but didn't want to get close enough to find out. It was possible that H had merely been showing off when she went out to the storeroom before dinner with a rolled-up newspaper to ward off black widows, but she seemed quite matter-of-fact, and the paper was kept all rolled and ready for her, on a shelf near the door. I felt more alien last night than I did in Sicily six years ago when an armed guard was patrolling the campground outside our tent. I know the altitude is supposed to make people sleepy, but it didn't work for me.

I must have slept for a while at least, because otherwise Tomas couldn't have woken me up. It was 6:30 when he came in and stood by my bed, looking at me with his long gray-green eyes that curve into points at the corners, just like mine. (Like poison-ivy leaves, N says.) His hair is sun-streaked and cut in the style of Christopher Robin's. "Hi, Anne," he said. "You sure are lazy."

I sat up and reminded myself to smile. I don't suppose I would like being called Aunt anyway. "What's that?" He was carrying a gun.

"Oh, just my gun." He seemed male, amused, tolerant.

"I see."

Tomas meets people's eyes much too easily, I can't help thinking. However, I am aware of my own prejudices against guns, overconfident children, and people with affected foreign names.

"Why do elephants wear glasses?" He leaned the gun against the end of the bed.

"What? But they don't." I was confused.

"To make sure they don't step on other elephants. Don't you remember?"

"Oh. It's a joke." I sent him that elephant book myself, last Christmas. He had a right to expect me to know what was in it.

"I heard you were sick before." He sat on the bed and looked at me with an interested expression. "What was wrong with you?"

"Oh, bronchitis."

He seemed disappointed. "Bronchitis! I've had that. Thousands of times. It can't kill you."

"Well, it kept coming back, and then I had pneumonia too," I said modestly.

He was impressed. "That can kill you. How high was your fever? I had a hundred and five and a half once when I was a baby. *And* convulsions."

"Only a hundred and three. And no convulsions."

"You get stiff, and your eyes roll up, and you froth at the mouth. My mother was scared out of her wits."

"I should think so." He is still young enough to be at my mercy. I can choose to be his friend or his enemy, and there won't be a thing he can do about it. I looked up at the blue and white doll then and saw that the black shape was only a curved, saw-toothed design of some sort, part of the doll's costume.

Tomas noticed what I was looking at. "From my birthday party," he said. "Cool, isn't it? Did you ever see a Batman piñata before?"

Never, I told him.

"Have you seen a rattlesnake yet?" Tomas asked me, just before I got him and his gun out of the room. How could he have guessed my most secret fear about coming here? I am not the kind of person who inspects snakes to see if they have little pits above their eyes before running away; to me, all snakes are poisonous. Like all spiders.

I dreamed about New Mexico before I came here—a month or so ago, when I still thought N was coming too. There was a deep blue sky, I remember, and I was walking along a narrow path cut into reddish rock. It wasn't like any place I had ever been, but I can still visualize it clearly. So now I have at least two New Mexicos in my mind—the one I expected to see and imagined H living in and the one I have seen since I got here yesterday. I catch myself picturing H's house as I thought of it when N and I first decided to come here, and then I have to tell myself that there's no such place: *there* is *here*. The real sky is as bright a blue sometimes as the sky on picture postcards, but the earth here is more tan than red. Utah is the place for red rocks, H says.

Dishonesty is creeping in already. I catch myself writing about the landscape—or starting to—as if I liked it, whereas really it isn't anything to like or dislike. It's here, and it's overwhelming and savage, and the truth is that it makes me want to crawl back under the covers. Maybe I was wrong in thinking of New Mexico as a refuge, but that's what it has to be for now.

Evening

I stayed in my room, writing, for a while after Tomas left. The activity in the kitchen sounded too hectic to face, and I had a strange, tight feeling in my head. My ears buzzed musically, and my face felt hot and pink, though when I looked in the mirror it seemed as pale as ever.

The voices next door began to say things like "What time is it?" "Who stole my math book?" and "Hurry up, dummy. We'll miss the bus." I went into the kitchen in time to see the three children run across the *portal* and down the path in the bright sunshine. Brown legs and pale hair and vivid, ragged clothes.

"Well, they're off." H turned away from the doorway. She was barefoot and wore the same Mexican blouse and long striped skirt she had on yesterday. I wonder whether it's really possible for an adult's eyes to change in color. H's eyes have always been more hazel than brown, but now they look even lighter, almost yellow. The skin at the outer corners is crumpled, too. The clear, unflattering light is partly to blame for that, probably; the contrast between light and shadow is so strong that when I look at my own reflection I notice lines in my forehead that seem new but must have been there for years, waiting to be discovered under Southwestern light.

H is thinner than I remembered. The shadows of ribs show along with her collar bones above the heavy lace at the top of her blouse, and her face seems narrower. Her shoulders slump in a way that reminds me of Mother, and she doesn't bother to hold her stomach in any more. I recalled my impression of yesterday—H radiant in the doorway with the children—and was confused. Either I had been wrong then or I was wrong now. Or both. I realized I was staring. "The children are so blond," I said, to imply that I had only been noticing the contrast between H's coloring and theirs.

She pulled a blue chair toward the orange table and sat down. "Yes, poor things. I wish they didn't look so Anglo. They get picked on at school."

Anglo. Of course. Not as bad as WASP, anyway. "Are most of their friends Mexican?"

"Don't say that." She looked stern. "Never say Mexican. People here, if they aren't Anglos or Indians, are Spanish, and they can't stand being called Mexicans."

"Yes. Well, I can see their point." More rules and new ways of offending people.

H was stirring her coffee. "Well. Where's Nat? What made him change his mind?"

"He couldn't get away." I knew she would ask. "Is Seth working already?" I made a gesture that included the kitchen walls, hung with dark wooden slabs encrusted with intricate metal designs. Not paintings, though H calls them that and Seth still refers to himself as a painter. The last time I saw him, he was turning out enormous canvases covered with small squares in checkerboard patterns, all alike except for the colors, as far as I could see. I didn't dare to question him about the paintings then because he had begun the conversation with a stream of abuse directed against people who couldn't see what his work was trying to say. And it has been exhibited and sold enough since to make me respectful. There's even a rumor that he's about to sell something to the Museum of Modern Art. I think I like this recent phase better than earlier ones. There is something pleasingly rustic about the large board that hangs against the white wall above the kitchen table, like a weathered barn door with interesting hinges. But am I supposed to see more in it than that? Yes, clearly.

"Oh, yes, he's working," H said. "The morning light, you know."

When I opened the cupboard to look for a cup, I was prepared to find sea kelp and safflower oil but saw instead that it was filled with cereals and cans and cake mixes. "What, no soy flour?" I said, then wished I hadn't.

H wasn't offended. "Not at the moment. The man at the health food store has started giving out pamphlets for the John Birch Society. He always seemed like such a nice man, and now it turns out he's a nut. He'll lose all his business. None of the Birchers will touch anything he sells."

"Steak and real butter and lots of California grapes."

"That's right. Cholesterol by the pound. But what's wrong with grapes? They're full of vitamin C."

There must be a time lag of some sort. My friends in the East have been boycotting grapes for two years in spite of their children's pleas. Last night I had to explain to H what "camp" meant, and I couldn't go through that again. "Nothing," I said.

H gathered up the breakfast dishes while I sat and watched her. The morning light was certainly unlike sunlight as I am used to it. It poured in through the window and made a still life out of the things on the table—the willow pattern cups and bowls, the bulbous blue-glass vase with a few wild flowers stuck into its narrow neck, the cut loaf of bread on its striped wooden board, even the stick of margarine dotted with crumbs and smears of jam. The curtains at the kitchen window are made from a cheap pumpkin-yellow material I would never have thought of choosing and that is just right. I watched H put on a long blue apron and tried to understand the disappointment mixed with the pleasure I feel at being with my sister again.

Because there is pleasure. There are still family sayings and references that only we can laugh at, and there is a way of looking at things that outsiders, even husbands, don't always understand. I've come to think lately that H and I were brought up rather like Victorian young ladies, with the same accomplishments and resources and only a few more. When we played the piano and sang together, for instance, we confined ourselves mainly to Gilbert and Sullivan or selections from *Songs the Whole World Sings*. A little Gershwin, sometimes, when we felt in a more modern mood, but that was as far as we went. Neither of us ever knew the words to popular songs or enjoyed listening to popular singers. We dismissed Elvis Presley as a commercial product with an ugly mouth; we preferred George London. For entertainment we went on bicycle or sketching trips together, and the family read Dickens aloud in the evenings. The books we read to ourselves, and we read a great deal, were nearly all English and at least 50 years old: E. Nesbit, Conan Doyle, Kipling, Lewis Carroll (even *Sylvie and Bruno*). Later on we graduated through Jeffery Farnol and Margaret Kennedy to Evelyn Waugh, Henry Green, Angus Wilson—none of whom helped very much in preparing us to live in the modern American world. We were, of course, involved in some of our father's church projects, but at the time we were growing up these tended to be innocuous—signing up donors for the blood bank, making aprons for the church fair, or taking May baskets to shut-ins. Even the Unitarian church didn't concern itself then with the draft or abortion-law reform.

"They might just as well have brought us up on an island," H said to me once, "and named us both Miranda."

Neither of us, still, can make a telephone call without becoming aware of our heartbeats, and I suspect we are both more anxious than most normal people when driving a car. We have never felt normal; that's the trouble. Superior sometimes and often inadequate, but never exactly normal. H's beauty and strong personality should have helped her to enter a world outside the parsonage, but I suppose it was too late by the time she began to go out with boys. She certainly saw a great many movies, but with a taste formed by the kind of reading she had done, how could she take most movies seriously? And the boys who took her to see them were awkward and pimpled and not enough like Mr. Knightley. She didn't even like most of the boys she went out with, she confided to me, but the practice might be useful afterwards when she was an actress.

Later, when H was away at college and after that when she was working at the Community Playhouse in a town in western Massachusetts, she had more complicated adventures. At college she was in love at least twice to my knowledge, both times with men that at the last minute she couldn't quite bring herself to agree to marry. There are two summer vacations I remember that vibrated with long-distance phone calls and special-delivery letters that left her crying in her room or carrying on mysterious conversations with Father behind the closed door of his study. And then in her second year at the Playhouse H met a director, a middle-aged married man who singled her out to conduct a very public affair with (in what sense of the term I have never been sure) in front of the whole Playhouse staff—sitting with her in coffee breaks, putting his arm around her at rehearsals—for about three months, long enough to persuade her that his marriage was unsuccessful only because he had been foolish enough to marry a registered nurse. He dropped H abruptly in January. He was insulting when she tried to approach him privately, she told me, and when he saw her in the company of other people he greeted the others but didn't look at H. At the time I was still sure of my sister's future as an actress. She hadn't ever meant to get married anyway, had she? And if she had, there were plenty of chances; suitors lurked around the house whenever she was home, and the long-distance calls continued. She was doing well at the Playhouse too, after the episode that the more experienced people there assured her was a sign of a promising future; in March she played Consuelo in *He Who Gets Slapped,* and in May she was Juliet.

I looked at my sister this morning, standing in the sunlight and washing the dishes and singing to herself, once again pretty as a picture. I realized then, to my shame, that I was almost as dismayed by her contentment as I had been by her depression seven years ago. Either way, it seemed to me, she was wasting her life. Wrong and unrealistic as I knew it was, I couldn't help feeling disappointed at finding H satisfied with a life so different from the one we had planned together for her. I almost felt that someone ought to rescue her.

May 25

A party last night, the first of the season, H says. "Everything happens in the summer here. In winter we all work and nobody sees anybody."

I wished I could get out of going. I wasn't feeling strong enough to carry the responsibility of being H's sister, and I didn't have anything to wear to the sort of party it was bound to be. The anemic flowered cotton? The light blue tailored suit? Never. The green linen shift was the only possibility, and I knew my legs weren't tan enough for it yet. I wouldn't be able to look like anything but a minor faculty wife dressed up for the Dean's tea at a small liberal arts college in upstate New York. "All you need is white gloves," H said. When I stood at the mirror, I saw that it wasn't only my clothes that were wrong; something had happened to my hair. This short, irregular cut is supposed to camouflage my rather strong features and draw attention to the shape of my eyes, but it has stopped doing anything of the sort. My hair began to go limp before I left Oklahoma, and last night it was hanging in meaningless wisps, as if it had been chopped off in some medical emergency. I looked stark and panic-stricken, and I felt plainer than I had for a long time.

A conversation with my host at the beginning of the party did nothing to restore my confidence. Bronson McKinney is a tall, melancholy man, reputedly a poet. He has colorless, longish hair and colorless eyes that turn down at the outer corners like the other lines in his face, and the general effect is one of nasty, sardonic attractiveness. "So you're the famous sister," he said, looking weary.

If H really had been talking about me to this man, I certainly didn't want to ask him what she had said. A comment on his house, which was overwhelming, would be too obvious, I felt, and H had gone off and left me. "I hear you're a poet. What are you working on now?" I was dismayed to hear myself ask.

Bronson continued to look at me, and the lines around his eyes got deeper. "I'm working on myself," he said in his prep school voice.

Was there any possible response to that? As soon as I

saw Bronson, I had known in my heart that he was the sort of man with whom small talk is impossible. Not that I am spectacular at it myself. I wished he wouldn't keep looking at me so hard. From his expression, I could see that he thought I ought to be working on myself, too.

"Your sister talks about you a lot," he said finally. He clearly disapproved of what he had heard.

"I see," I think I said.

"She admires you," he said in an unbelieving tone.

"Really?" I was more surprised than he was. "Well, there's no accounting for tastes."

"I hear you're supposed to have had pneumonia." He was still staring at me. "Don't you know there's no such thing?"

"What do you mean? Of course there is." I could only think he must be a Christian Scientist or something similar but more modern.

"Not as far as you're concerned. It's all in your mind." He directed his knowing little eyes down at me, looking pleased at being able to let me see that he had classified me as a frigid lady with hysterical symptoms.

An amateur Freudian then. I have had more than enough of that lately. So much, in fact, that I felt almost triumphant when the doctor insisted on showing N my X-rays. I didn't have them with me last night, however.

"Guilt can do strange things," Bronson said.

"What?" I thought I must have missed something he had just said.

"Funny how some people like to think of themselves as writers. You're not a writer."

"No," I said. "Certainly not." Had I said I was?

"You don't work at it. You don't even know what it is to live." He spoke calmly, still looking pleased.

I looked desperately for H. Then I noticed the printing press against the wall behind Bronson and remembered that H had said that he printed his own poems. "Which typefaces do you use?" I asked.

"Baskerville mainly. Some Garamond." He dropped his ironic expression and simply answered my question.

"Yes. I remember those. Tell me some more names. Centaur. Do you use that? Or Deepdene?"

"Too beautiful. Distracting if you're printing anything longer than a page. Bodoni, Gothic, Goudy—you wouldn't like those much." He was looking almost friendly.

"Bodoni sounds lovely. Like lace or something very delicate to eat." I wondered whether I should tell him about the time N and I almost bought a hand press.

"It isn't. It's useful, but you wouldn't like it particularly." That sounded almost like a compliment, as if he took my good taste for granted. "How about Century Schoolbook?"

"Ugh."

"Better than Bodoni." He smiled at me, but I must have been wearing the wrong expression because suddenly his whole face drooped into a set of downward lines. "Don't pretend to be interested. What's the point?" He walked away to the other end of the room.

I stood alone, feeling bruised. I have never been any good at games.

I saw a tall man with a weathered face and a little blond beard approaching. Oh no, I thought, not another one, and fled toward a circle of people where I saw H. But then I noticed Bronson McKinney standing next to her and turned away again. The other man, I saw with despair, was too close now to escape from with any subtlety. I sank onto a couch.

"You're Harriet's sister," the man said reverently, bending down toward the very low couch I was sitting on and taking my hand as though he might be going to kiss it. He was about forty, with enthusiastic eyes. "The Writer," he said. He kept hold of my hand and knelt in front of me.

The room appeared to be full of embarrassing men, though this one seemed friendly. I pulled my hand away on the pretext of having to move over and make room for him. "Not really," I said.

He was still kneeling and looking into my eyes. "Anna. That's your name."

"Just Anne." But I thought how interesting it might be to be Anna the Writer.

He sat down in a cross-legged position on the dirt floor. "I'm Kurt," he said, and looked expectant.

"Oh. Hello." I couldn't remember H mentioning anyone named Kurt.

"What do you think of our scenery?" He was looking at me as if my answer would be important to him.

"I'm not sure yet."

"So you don't like it." Kurt seemed prepared to accept my judgment and regulate his own opinion accordingly, as if I were a well-known scenery critic.

"Please. I didn't say that. It's beautiful." He nodded, looking flattered. "It just isn't . . . manageable." He was still nodding. Not another Bronson after all. "One thing I noticed on the drive here," I said, "was the way the trees got smaller. I never thought about it before, but there are some very tall trees in the East. They diminish as you drive west until by the time you get here, they aren't very important any more."

He was still looking at me. "Anna," he said dreamily.

"New England is vertical," I decided, "and the Southwest is horizontal."

He looked at me with the same smile. "Anna."

"Yes." I was excited by the idea, as I always am on finding it possible to define something. "Of course, there are the mountains and gorges, but it's still horizontal." But I was explaining too much, and he wasn't listening.

"Harriet is one of the most beautiful women I know," he said, "and one of the most brilliant."

I was pleased. "Yes."

"Just to walk into her house, to see her with her children, to sense that serene feminine atmosphere, you don't know what it does for me." He leaned forward. "Have you ever watched her hanging up laundry? The line of her arms, the colors in her hair and skin, that delicate curve at the side of her face when her head is thrown back?"

This man seemed to be in love with H. Why hadn't she mentioned him? "Yes," I said. "I've always liked to watch Harriet."

"Just what I mean!" He studied my face. "You're nothing like your sister, are you?"

He probably wasn't trying to hurt my feelings. Besides, it was true. "No, I suppose not," I said.

"A different and very rare kind of beauty."

Oh. Maybe he thought everyone was beautiful. How nice for him.

"More remote," he said. "The same hair, but your

eyes aren't like hers. I've been watching you as you look at the people in this room, and I can tell that you see them with a novelist's eye."

"How could anyone possibly tell a thing like that?"

"I can tell. I'm a painter, you know." He glanced toward a picture that hung above the curved adobe fireplace below two crossed rifles. It was too far away for me to see clearly.

"Did Harriet say I was a writer?"

"She's very proud of you, talks about you all the time."

"Oh." Maybe she does. My notoriety during the past year has almost accustomed me to the idea that people might talk about me. ("I just wanted you to know that I don't believe what everyone's saying about you," one of my friends called to say.) But not H. "I'm not really, you know. I did get something published, but it wasn't serious. If I'm anything, I'm a librarian." But he was looking at me with the same rapt expression he had when he was talking about H hanging up laundry.

It was strange being Beautiful Anna. N likes my looks, I think, but, "beautiful" is not a word he would apply to me. The closest he ever came, that I can remember, was one time when I had rushed in from some kind of stimulating outdoor activity–raking leaves or picketing or something–and he told me I reminded him of Rudolf Nureyev. I was flattered; mostly he thinks I look more like Julia Child.

I was feeling very light-headed last night–partly altitude, I'm sure, but some of the feeling came from the bright colors in the room and some of it from the room itself. The McKinneys' house is an enormous oval igloo made of adobe bricks. Bronson McKinney designed and built it himself. There is a thick, peeled tree trunk in the center of the floor, going all the way up to support the ceiling beams that radiate from it. The only windows are two big, many-paned ones set into the wall after it begins to slant in. Skylights, really, one above the bed and the other next to the table, and both placed, H says, to show mountain ranges (which I couldn't see because it was dark, but I think I can imagine). Bronson's printing press and type stand are near his wife's loom, along with book-binding equipment. The most interesting room I've been in, I think, and full of things that people use. Ivory chessmen on a board (no plastic allowed in the house, I bet), a telescope pointed toward one of the windows, all sorts of tin or enameled cooking utensils that I couldn't identify. There was a pump organ with pleated rose silk in the top and a child's piano book (John Thompson, *Teaching Little Fingers to Play*) on the music rack and a guitar leaning against it. Two swings hung from the beams near the fireplace, and at least five homemade kites dangled like mobiles. Gerbils in a cage, a fairly large lime tree with limes, in front of the fireplace an armchair with its legs sawed off. There was also a sleek new wall oven, the first I've seen set into an unplastered adobe wall. The rugs, curtains, and cushion covers were, of course, all woven by Gretchen McKinney.

The people there last night were as unfamiliar as anything else in the room. They looked a lot like many of the people I'm used to seeing on campuses or at peace rallies. The room was full of Indian jewelry, Levis, work shirts, unbleached muslin dresses, sandals, moccasins, and cowboy boots. Everyone there must be either an artist or a political protester, I thought when I first saw them, but I was wrong. There was one woman, for instance, who looked exactly like the most reliable member of a church Social Concerns Committee, the sort of person who carries around petitions so reasonable that you read them before signing only because she would disapprove if you didn't. I saw her talking energetically to a pretty dark girl in a way that could only mean she was in favor of legalizing abortion or getting out of Vietnam, but as I came closer I heard the woman say, in tones of horror, "Do you mean to say you feed your children *pasteurized* milk?"

Now the same woman came and sat on the couch next to Kurt and leaned across him to talk to me. I still expected her to be interested in politics, but all she would talk about was Adelle Davis. "How many children have you, my dear?" she asked me. When I told her I had none, she looked compassionate and leaned toward me across Kurt's lap. "The sure-fire way to get pregnant," she said, "is to take lots of Vitamin E." She patted Kurt's knee. "Sure-fire!"

I didn't look at Kurt. "But suppose I don't want to? Suppose I think there are already enough people in the world?"

"Oh, no one could think that. I mean, it may be true in India or somewhere, but people don't apply an abstract idea like that to themselves, now do they?"

"I do."

She smiled reassuringly. "Vitamin E, now don't forget." She patted Kurt's knee again and left.

Kurt stayed near me for the rest of the evening, and I kept wondering how soon he would start to see through me. I know it's my own fault if people sometimes start out thinking I'm a more interesting person than I really am. It comes of my habit of pretending, if I feel insecure, that I am someone else. Be Harriet, I tell myself, or Simone de Beauvoir, or Katharine Hepburn. It seems to work for the first few minutes, but I don't have enough conviction to keep up the pretense, and people are nearly always disillusioned soon. Not Kurt, though. Last night I didn't even have to create my own characterization. I was a promising young novelist called Anna, part Italian, perhaps, or Swedish. It was rather fun. "Did you really paint that picture?" I asked him, and walked toward the fireplace.

"Gretchen," he said when we were close enough to see the painting. It was a portrait of a woman sitting at a loom, her hands and arms drawn in more detail than her blurred, serious face. The style, with blue-green shadows and orange highlights, made me think of the early German Expressionists. I looked around automatically for the real Gretchen McKinney.

She sat near the loom that appeared in the picture, at one end of the large oval room. I thought of her at first as sitting in the corner until I reminded myself that the room had no corners. Gretchen is just as impressive and unreachable as anything in her house. She has blond braids, round brown eyes (Italian madonna), and a German accent just pronounced enough to be an asset. She was wearing one of those dirndls with the white blouse and tight black bodice and flowered skirt. She seemed not to react to anything I said when I met her, though there was no question of her not understanding me. In the car going home H said Gretchen was shy. That may be, but there are more appealing ways of being shy than sighing when someone praises your rugs. Actually, I can't blame her for that now. H explained that Gretchen is tired of having a dirt floor when Bronson has promised for years to put in an adobe one, and she's annoyed about dirt getting ground into her handwoven rugs.

(Must find out the difference between dirt and adobe floors.)

The McKinneys have no running water but do have an adobe outhouse with stained-glass windows—also a swimming pool that uses water from an irrigation ditch. When they want to empty it, one of their children dives to the bottom and pulls out a giant plug, and the water runs out through a tube in the side into their garden.

Does Bronson McKinney treat everyone that way? I kept looking around for N to come and save me.

I hope Bronson's poetry is no good.

A young couple, the Ortegas—Angela and Luis—were the only Spanish people there last night and the only guests who seemed to be as much out of place as I was. Both handsome—she soft and pretty in a starched pink shirtwaist dress, he fierce and primitive. I didn't have a chance to talk much with them.

Conversation on the way home in the truck, me sitting between H and S and trying not to be pushed against's S's warm, spreading thigh, though feeling foolish because he doesn't know I am there anyway.

H: What did you think of Kurt?

I: (cautiously, not knowing what the situation may be between K and my sister) He seemed very nice. (S laughs scornfully, as if I didn't know how prim I sound.) Is he always so enthusiastic, or had he been drinking? I mean, was that his usual self?

S: Sounds like his usual self.

I: I didn't know whether to take him seriously.

H: Always take Kurt seriously.

Now what does that mean? She is in one of her Down moods now, staring at her hands, though at the party she charmed everyone. "He's insane, you know," she says suddenly, "but I don't know what we'd all do without him."

"A damn good painter," Seth grunts, and we don't say anything more till we're home.

May 26

I was wrong about H being happy. She followed me into my room when I came to make my bed. She was wearing the same clothes for the third day in a row, and I remembered that in the past this was always a bad sign. (Why must I seize on these details? I see what N means about my being petty.) Sometimes she would wear a dress for over a week, or as long as she could get away with it, as a signal, I think, that she was depressed and wanted to be treated kindly. It used to infuriate Mother, who assumed either that H was lazy or that she was hinting for new clothes. Father never noticed, and if Mother drew his attention to H, he just nodded like one of the Cheeryble brothers and said "Very charming, my dear."

H sat on the bed right away and started to tell me about Seth. He cares for nothing but his career, she says, and he sees her as a hindrance because she doesn't do enough to promote it. He wants her to be a hostess and help him to impress influential people. "I should think you'd be good at that," I said, and she agreed that she was, but not good enough to please Seth. And he resents the time she gives to the children. She and Seth throw plates at each other—have used up almost all their Russel Wright seafoam-blue wedding-present dishes by smashing them against the wall. Usually they duck and the wall gets dented; she showed me places where the paint is chipped off. She sounded very calm while she was telling me this, amused at my inexperience though at the same time taking it for granted that my marriage was as bad as hers if I would only tell her about it. (I swear I won't.) Seth won't pay attention to her, she says. Which sounded like a contradiction after she told me about the plate-throwing. But what she means is that he won't discuss anything. Either fights in a violent way or locks himself in his studio alone. He didn't come to the hospital when Tomas was born—was too busy building a crate for a big painting he wanted to ship off that day. And H had a hemorrhage and almost died, but he was so annoyed with her for being pregnant in the first place that a friend had to drive her and the baby home. She kept giving little laughs while she told me this, as if these were jolly domestic stories that I might enjoy.

H and Mother quarreled all through my childhood, but now they remind me of each other. Mother used to talk about Father in just H's tone, with that same slight laugh, when there was something he had done or (usually) failed to do. Forgotten to pick her up at the bus station or called on a parishioner and stayed for dinner without letting her know. We had lots of family anecdotes like that, with Mother the amused martyr. Still, I can't see Father throwing dishes.

Then Seth came in. The beast, the terrible brute who has ruined my beautiful sister's life. I was startled and couldn't speak to him. "Have you stopped beating your wife?" was the only thing that came into my mind.

"Hi," he said, looking as mild and stodgy as he always does, even when discussing art critics. He didn't bother to smile, and I was certain that he was about to guess just what we'd been talking about.

Finally I said "Good morning," in a strangled, formal voice.

"Hi, darling," H said, leaning back on her elbows on my unmade bed. "How's it going?"

The rest of the conversation was ordinary husband-and-wife chatter. Seth had run out of solder or finishing nails or something, and H asked him to pick up some milk on his way back from town. He offered to take me and show me the sights, and H actually urged me to go, but I couldn't bear to. When he had left, I looked at H questioningly, and she just raised her eyebrows and said, "Well, life has to go on," then paused and said, "I guess."

Evening

No word from N. It hasn't been very long, but I thought I would have heard from him by now or that he would be here. H wonders. I do too.

H tried to explain Bronson McKinney to me today. She was surprised to hear he'd been rude to me, had thought we would get along beautifully. This information depressed me, as I always hate finding that other people like someone I can't get along with at all. It only confirmed the feeling I had at the party that he was singling me out, for no good reason, to attack in a way that other people wouldn't notice.

He is a poet, but a failed one, it seems, and my question about his writing was even more inept than it seemed to me as soon as I asked it. "He hasn't finished anything for a long time," H told me. "Gretchen doesn't think so, anyway, though she doesn't dare ask."

"No, I can see she wouldn't. But how does she know?"

"She goes through his papers when he isn't home. Gretchen is so unsubtle. She's always pushing Bronson, trying to help him. She keeps offering to set type for him, when she ought to know from her spying that he hasn't written a poem for a year."

"What does he do then?"

"Builds bathtubs."

"What?"

"Not ordinary bathtubs. But ours, for instance. It's the first one he ever did, and he built it in exchange for a painting by the owner of this house. After he went into the business, his bathtubs got even more elaborate. They're made of those little colored tiles in lovely designs, with the faucets in much more logical places than the usual ones. He designs them individually to the measurements of his customers and charges thousands of dollars."

"But does anyone buy them?"

"Absolutely. Rich people. Not that he needs the money. He's the heir to a brassiere fortune, you know."

"Oh. *Those* McKinneys." Poor, rich Bronson.

"The McKinneys don't have to worry about starving between bathtub commissions. He's built them mostly for Texans so far, but he had an offer from New York last fall, and he's going to be featured in an article in *Craft Horizons*. As a bathtub designer he's a genius, but unfortunately he thinks he ought to be a poet."

"And Gretchen wants to be married to a poet."

"That's what he was when she married him. She gave up her painting because he said it interfered with his writing, and now he still doesn't write."

"She shouldn't have given it up."

"She didn't know he was only looking for an excuse." H's golden eyes looked out of the window toward the mountains. "Gretchen used to do the most charming watercolors. But if Bronson was rude the other night, you can see why."

I can see partly why. When Bronson accused me of pretending to be a writer, maybe he was talking about himself. He might even be envious of what he may consider my success. Still, I can't feel much sympathy for him.

I asked H's advice today about finding a place to live. I can't keep staying here and crowding Tomas out of his room. A cottage for rent? A motel? I had no idea what might be available. "Can you afford to pay rent?" H asked me. It turns out that she and Seth have never had to pay for any of the houses they've lived in here. "It's a good thing too," she said, "because we couldn't."

I knew we were headed for one of those conversations in which H contrasts the opulence of my life with the squalor of hers. I don't know how she imagines N and I live, but things like opera tickets, wine for dinner, and tourist-class trips to Europe—things that are a normal part of faculty life these days—are to H such impossible luxuries that they must seem like signs of wealth. She can't help feeling some resentment. I suppose neither of us has gotten over expecting life to be fair. I remember her thank-you note one Christmas when I had been overgenerous: "Your

CARE package saved us. The simple life is all very well for grown-up people (including me? sometimes I wonder), but the truth is that children love getting presents that aren't homemade. You should have seen the way they swarmed over those bakery gingerbread men and all the nice commercial games, ignoring the doll clothes and stuffed animals I've been slaving over for months. Well, that's the way it is when you're poor. Anyway, thank you more than I can say."

The awkwardness about money has become worse since *Household* published my novelette. But if I told H and Seth that I've made only a few hundred dollars from it and am not likely to earn any more unless some publisher loses his mind and snaps up the paper-back rights, the disillusionment would be too cruel. Seth has been selling paintings, when he sells them, for much more than that.

"There are disadvantages in caretaking, of course," H said. "Such as having to move sometimes at very short notice. And having the roof of the *portal* col-lapse because the owner hasn't seen it in twelve years and doesn't know it needs fixing. And Seth, of course, in spite of having to learn about carpentry because of the kind of paintings he's doing, wouldn't deign to fix a mere roof. Especially when it belongs to somebody else."

"No, I suppose not."

"And sometimes the walls are covered with pictures that aren't the kind you would choose to live with, or things like those guns hanging all over our living room when we moved in, or there are bugs. . . . Of course, most of these things can be true if you rent, too."

"Guns?" I thought I would have noticed those.

"I hid them behind the spices in the kitchen cupboard. I don't suppose they're loaded, but I wasn't absolutely sure how to find out."

I didn't say anything.

"This is a gun culture," H said. "You don't suppose I like it either, do you? If you tell a man around here that his gun is dangerous and a sign of insecurity and a phallic symbol as well, he'll just stare at you suggestively and ask you what makes you think it's a phallic symbol."

"But that's obvious."

"To you it is, and to me. Not to some man whose most precious possession is the right to bear arms."

She took me to see Kurt, whose house she had heard was for rent. We drove through the center of town and down a potholed blacktop road past Montoya's Radio Repair, Big Brad's Pizza, and a few other small adobe stores, and we were out in the country, with pink houses on a hill on the right and a grassy field on the left, with three horses posing on the other side of a fence near a group of cottonwood trees. Lower Ranchitos. There was a bar and a pool hall at the side of the road, white and battered, with peeling paint that showed through in places to crumbling brown bricks. It's interesting the way unplastered adobe loses its shape and gradually sinks back into the ground. One of the ruined buildings we passed in the center of town had nothing left but a few low, irregular walls, about as solid-looking as a children's sand fortress, and yet H says an adobe house will last forever if it's plastered regularly.

We drove down a steep dirt road and crossed a rough log bridge over a stream—Rio Pueblo, fed by snow water from the mountains. We could see Kurt's house about a hundred yards ahead, at the end of a complicated system of roads and fences. "Kurt shares this entrance with the Ortegas," H explained. "He has a road of his own, but he doesn't bother to keep it in repair. It's simpler to have just one road to the two houses, and Kurt takes care of filling up the ruts. It works fine as long as they stay friendly."

"What if they don't?"

"He'd have to use his own road, I guess. It's not likely. Though you can't tell; Luis is funny."

"Oh. Luis. They were at the party."

"Kurt must have brought them. He's been trying to introduce Angie into the social life of the artists. He's right, of course; there should be more contact between the different groups of people in town, and Angie is so bright, really. She may be the only Spanish person in town with a library card. But Luis just feels uncomfortable with people like the McKinneys. It's all right for him to take Kurt fishing, but a house like the McKinneys'—dirt floor and no plumbing—shocks him, especially when he knows they could afford hardwood floors like the ones he wants for his house."

Kurt's house is small and square, with two blue-framed windows and a faded blue door set into the sloping unpainted adobe wall like the eye and mouth holes in a primitive mask that might be used by a dancer impersonating some friendly animal. H parked the truck at the end of a path, and we made our way through aromatic waist-high weeds, past a battered outhouse and a small grove of fruit trees. H knocked on the deep-set blue door. I hadn't seen a natural adobe wall at such close range before, and I noticed that the surface of the house was criss-crossed with shallow, wavering cracks like those in the mud of a dried puddle. There were small round holes every few inches, and I saw what looked like an emerald-green bee crawl out of one of them and fly away toward the trees. Then a scarlet bee came out of another hole. I could feel sunlight pressing like a solid, hot weight at the back of my head, and when I turned and looked toward the truck, the flash of reflected light from the chrome trimmings hurt my eyes and repeated itself in the air for a minute afterwards. H leaned into the door and knocked on it again. "He's probably meditating," she said.

The door opened, and Kurt stood there beaming at us. We stepped into a long, cool room like a deep cave, divided by a partition into two sections. There was a smell of turpentine, kerosene, and something else, possibly scented soap. The two windows in the front of the house provided the only light in the first room. There was a three-burner kerosene stove in a corner near one window, with a print of one of Raphael's madonnas above it and a plastic rosary suspended from a nail. Next to that was a framed picture of an ornamented purple elephant. The rest of the scarred whitewashed wall was hung with saucepans and stirring spoons and several paintings that I recognized as being in Kurt's style. A wooden packing case, the top painted orange, served as a counter. Shelves of rough wood held dishes and cans of food, and racks overhead were filled with stretched canvases. The floor was covered with loose pieces of linoleum with the pattern almost worn off.

The room on the other side of the partition was dominated by a six-foot-square window in the far wall.

A double mattress covered with an Indian rug lay on the floor in a corner under a rack of paintings, and a small kerosene heating stove stood against the wall near the window. Several metal trunks were ranged near it in a conversational group, with folded blankets draped over their trops. In this room the linoleum was covered in most places by straw mats. The general impression was one of order. There were none of the ash-filled coffee cups, dropped socks, or grimy towels I associate with the rooms of men living by themselves.

Still, it was not the sort of house I was looking for. One of the neat pink bungalows near H's place was more what I had had in mind, with three little rooms, a porch across the front, a stairstep adobe fireplace, and running water. A bare light bulb hanging from the ceiling of each of the rooms here indicated that there was electricity, but nothing else about the house fitted in with my ideas. There was no fireplace at all, and no porch, and the ceiling must be twelve feet high. I looked up at the long sooty *vigas* above my head. They went with the big window, but they were too magnificent for me.

"Sit down," Kurt said, hovering and shining his eyes at us. "The most wonderful thing. I've just seen my father."

"Oh, Kurt, how exciting," H said. "Did he say anything?"

"No, he just floated there, with a sort of green glow around his head. Just about where you're standing, Anna." I tried not to move. "Let me get you some coffee." He went into the kitchen.

"His father is dead?" I asked H softly.

"Of course. How else could he appear with a green

glow around his head?" Her voice wavered in the last part of the question, I was glad to notice. "Kurt has been trying to get through to him for years."

I sat down on the window sill next to an incense burner that was giving off the smell I had identified as soap. I could see a green meadow beyond the tall weeds outside the window, a mesa in the distance. The window was divided into separate panes, two of them hinged and covered with screens. Both of these were open, and there was the sound of water running somewhere just outside. The irrigation ditch, H explained.

Though there are other houses close by on both sides, from the inside Kurt's house appears to be isolated. I couldn't see any other buildings from the back window at all, and in front there are just a few apricot-colored dwellings far away at the foot of the mountains. Even the cafe we passed at the corner is hidden by trees. Because of this and maybe because of the high ceiling and thick walls, the atmosphere is one of unusual peace.

May 27

Kurt's coffee cups: One yellow chipped enamel, one dimestore willow pattern, and a gold-rimmed bone-china teacup with a broken handle. It seemed like affectation, or at least like a criticism of people who have dishes that match. But Kurt doesn't criticize people. (Must remember that and stop being defensive because of suspecting irony.)

I couldn't help seeing the house as it might be, with the picture racks taken down and bookcases and a fireplace put in. As H says, the vibrations are good; the house feels right, spacious but snug.

And I must move out of here before H and I say things to each other that can't be taken back. I can't stay with her any more comfortably than I could with Mother and Father this spring.

Breakfast with my parents in April in the windy, white-turreted fishing village where they live now: My mother tries to make me eat an egg because I look thin. I want to look thin, I don't tell her; is there anybody who wants to look fat? They question me about N. I tell them he is busy revising the Dickens book, and they stop as respectfully as I knew they would when I planned what to say. We expect to take our western trip, I tell them, as soon as N can finish his work. (Though he has been on leave since January, I am still hoping then that what I am saying is true.) I wish I could tell them what my troubles are and ask them what to do, but I have never been able to do that.

However, it seems that they have difficulties of their own. My father looks up from the current copy of the weekly bulletin of his former church, sent to him because he is minister emeritus. "Can anyone tell me," he asks, "what an encounter group might be?" I don't tell him, and my mother can't. The bulletin has changed its format, I notice; the heading is printed in vibrating pink and purple. My father studies it with an expression of anxious distaste. "I suppose he appeals to the young people," he manages to say.

But later, when we were walking into town together to get the morning paper, he asked me whether I was familiar with the works of Rod McKuen, whose poetry was reported to have been used in the last week's service, along with readings from the Song of Solomon and *Soul on Ice*, and I could see that he was angry.

"It sounds as though the church is running off madly in all directions," I said. I couldn't help wondering why it is that so many ministers seem to lack an aesthetic sense; I recalled a service my father had based on Robert Frost's poem "The Road Not Taken," even after H and I, full of adolescent disapproval, had tried to point out the contradiction and self-congratulation we could see in the poem. But this was much worse.

"Exactly." His natural cheerfulness came back then and he stalked into the wind, marching to his different drummer, while I tried to walk faster and felt my lips turning blue from lack of oxygen.

My poor father, voted out of his final job by a coalition of liberals and conservatives who could understand neither his integrity nor his sermons, and replaced by a young man in sideburns and medallions and an air of scattered optimism—my father walks those two miles to the newspaper store every day and comes back rejoicing in the headlines about student unrest, happy to see that someone else is finally noticing wrongs he has been pointing out for years. But he must be uneasy, too. He isn't deceived by what is happening in the churches; does he think that universities are populated by a superior race? How can anyone who has sat through a parish meeting, with all the rationalizing, the categorizing and refusals to listen ("Oh, the book *I* could write," my mother says.) believe in the inevitable trumph of good?

My poor father.

* * *

The trouble is, Kurt wants to sell the house, not rent it. And, unfortunately, it wouldn't be impossible for me to buy it. He's only asking $2,500, and I have more than that in the bank because of the book and my library salary for the last year.

H was in one of her manic moods when we were there, running around and pointing out how easy it would be to put a porch on the front and a terrace on the side and back, and though I see that it wouldn't be easy at all, still it would be possible. I have never lived in a house that was mine. Various parsonages when we were growing up, rented rooms before I was married, and then faculty housing. I suppose I must have some notion that owning a house might make me feel at home.

But there is no running water (although there is a sink with a drain), and I don't trust either the cooking stove or the heating one. I would have to work all summer to make the house look the way I see it in my mind, but that excites me rather, because it's work I could do myself. Surely after all the apartment walls I have scraped, spackled, sanded, painted, papered, I could learn mud-plastering.

I wish I knew what N would think.

Lilacs still blooming here, along the road next to the house. And Hollyhocks in everybody's gardens, including mine. Mine?

2

May 28

I am never reminded of the past so much as when I'm with H. She broods over it as if all her happiness were there and as if she could solve her present problems if only she could find past explanations for them.

And yet she gets things wrong.

There was a bitter, fierce fight between us at the dinner table tonight, with H's eyes blazing and my voice trembling and the children watching us in amazement because of the pettiness of the issue we were quarreling about.

The BB hole in the parsonage window. H insists it was in the dining room, through the stained-glass Easter lily, while I know it was in the window on the landing above the bench. Didn't I spend a large part of my youth sitting there and reading, stopping occasionally to run my finger around the faceted edge of the crater or to peer through the tiny circle in the center? And didn't I sit there just a year ago doing the same thing for part of an afternoon on my parents' last day in the house, listening to Mother's hints about the unworthiness of the new minister and his wife?

What happened tonight was that H found out that Tomas has been shooting at birds with his new BB gun. He claimed first never to have hit one, then said that BBs are harmless anyway, then that everybody shoots birds. H was upset, naturally, and told him about the little girl we knew who was shot in the eye, and then she mentioned the window.

I had sense enough not to contradict her when she started being dramatic about the hole in the dining-room window and how we had to see it at every meal when we were growing up and how it had given her a sense of insecurity that would last for the rest of her life. I wouldn't have said anything if she hadn't dragged me in.

"Didn't it give you the same feeling?" she asked me.

"Was there a hole in the dining-room window too?" I knew there wasn't, but I was willing to bargain.

"What do you mean *too?*" H uses her eyes for many other purposes besides seeing. When she said this, they looked yellow and she was glaring at me, attacking.

"Besides the one on the landing," I unforgivably said.

"There was only one hole, and it was in the dining room." She stood up, and I was afraid, after what she had told me about the usual fights in this house, that she might throw her bowl of chili at me.

She didn't, but the argument went on and of course I was angry too, and unfortunately she made some general accusations about my always having to be right and feeling superior, etc. If we had let it go further, we might have found out what we were really fighting about. Which might or might not have been a good thing.

I must decide. Either I drive back to New York, or I

take Kurt's house and move in right away. Any sensible, healthy person would be able to consider a less extreme possibility, but I am not healthy, and I'm getting tired of being sensible. Anyway, I must not stay here.

It's important that the right person live in the house, Kurt says, because of the vibrations. "Don't you see that this house is what you need?" he said. What he needs is my money, to pay for the new house he's building for himself near the Gorge.

But he is right, I feel, and I can't help being flattered at his approving of my vibrations. He wouldn't sell his house to just anybody, he implies.

May 28, 1969

Dear Nat—

Shall we buy a house?

I am serious. There is a beautiful house here, and it's for sale at a price we can afford. If I describe it to you completely, it won't sound beautiful, and if you came and looked at it and the weather happened to be bad or the light wrong, it wouldn't even be *beautiful. But it really is.*

Let me mention some of the good things: High ceiling, with straight, peeled tree trunks for beams. An enormous window that frames the most extraordinary sunsets they have anywhere. (Really. I swear it. The first time I saw one, I was afraid. Such a variety of changing colors and great towering mounds of clouds lighted from behind, with long sudden beams of light pointing through. I ran into the house and asked Harriet whether this might mean that the scientists at Los Alamos had just done something terrible. But no; the same thing happens every evening to some degree, and right outside that big window, with the silhouettes of trees and a mesa in front.)

The walls of the house are two feet thick. Three advantages here that I can think of: deep window sills you can sit in, insulation that keeps the temperature at 70, and a feeling of permanence and security.

The front door is blue, guaranteed to keep evil spirits away. There are lilacs, plum trees, mint, enough garlic (good against evil spirits too, or is it only vampires?) to flavor every salad we eat for the rest of our lives, and there is watercress on the edge of the stream at the end of our property. Did I tell you that there is a stream? Some little Spanish boys were fishing there with long poles when I went to see the house. They looked up at me with their round Japanese faces, and I suppose that by now everyone in the neighborhood knows that I came and why.

I won't tell you any of the drawbacks of the place because they would sound worse than they are.

My idea—not so impractical as it might seem at first—is that we should buy the house and fix it up to use for vacations. It might help with the feeling of not living anywhere that we've complained about so often. If we came here every summer, no matter what part of the country we might live in for the rest of the year, we would finally have a place that would be our house, with familiar scenery and friends. Because there are people here we would like to know—writers and artists who have moved here for the climate, mainly—and they would welcome us.

Please

May 29, 1969

Dear Nat—

I have done something that I tried, without succeeding, to write to you about yesterday. I couldn't finish the letter because I didn't know whether you were listening. Are you now? I thought I would have heard from you. Do you have Harriet's address? Or General Delivery would do.

I have agreed to buy a house. Strange, I know, but I think you would understand if you saw it. The price is low. Shall I tell you any more?

Love,
A.

May 29

"Isn't it splendid!" I remember my father saying that day in April on our walk home from the newspaper store. I don't know anyone else who would use an old-fashioned word like splendid. He was referring to the *Boston Globe*'s account of the student occupation of University Hall at Harvard.

"Could you slow down a little?" I said. My father makes a fine picture, with his bony, handsome face lifted into the wind and his pipe clenched between his teeth, but it's hard to keep up with him, especially when he's just received heartening news.

He stopped and handed me the folded paper. "There," he said, pointing to an article with his pipe. "The young people of today are the hope of the world."

"It says they forced the deans and secretaries out of their offices," I said. "They carried some of them down the stairs." It was hard to tell very much, standing there, of what had happened, and the paper didn't give enough details on the front page.

"Oh?" He frowned faintly. "I'll have to read the story more carefully when I get back to my study." But he plunged along then at his usual pace, almost singing with joy, and I was too touched by his happiness to argue. Also too much out of breath.

It was that morning, after I had learned about the Harvard takeover, that I first thought that N might not come here with me after all. What happens at Harvard can happen at other universities too. How could he leave his campus when, for the first time in his life, he could feel sure that it was the right place for him to be?

May 30

Moving day. When I was driving up to the house with Tomas in the front seat, I stopped just before crossing the river and put my letter to N inside Kurt's former mailbox and lifted the red flag. I was taking possession.

I had forgotten how comic the front of the house is; its naive, semi-human expression dismayed me a little. "Do you think the house looks funny?" I asked Tomas.

"What do you mean funny? It's Kurt's house," he said. Very reasonable.

Kurt met us at the door. He had packed up his possessions, but I was surprised to see how many things he had left for me. There is a round tin tub for baths and laundry, a saucepan, a frying pan, and enough heterogeneous dishes to serve two people. The mattress is still in a corner of the living room with a crude, carved table beside it, and one of the trunks stands next to the wall. It won't close properly, Kurt explained, but I can use it for storage. There is a Mexican blue-glass jug on the sill of the big window. The straw mats are still here, I was relieved to see, and there is one of Kurt's pictures on the kitchen wall—a street of crooked blue buildings with a white moon shining down. Another, larger painting hangs in the big room. It is done in tones of pink, orange, and gold, and shows a red-haired woman kneeling to embrace two children.

"I didn't know whether you'd want the paintings," Kurt said.

"To store for you, you mean?" I was cautious.

"No, to keep. They're yours if you want them. Take them down if you don't."

How kind he is. I was so touched that my face felt stiff when I thanked him, and I was afraid I might be looking ungrateful.

Records: almost entirely Bach and Mozart, except for Lotte Lenya and *Candide*.

Books: Emerson, Thoreau, Jane Austen, Proust, Shakespeare, Yeats, thesaurus, dictionary, *N.Y. Times Cookbook*, K. Mansfield's letters to J.M. Murry (My desert island books. *Robinson Crusoe* might have been useful.)

Miscellaneous things:

typewriter
typing paper
7 notebooks, mostly filled with incoherent writing
3 folders of typed passages that don't fit together
clipboard with "Anne Curtis" scratched into it at the top
alarm clock
sewing kit
leather-framed picture of N six years ago, wearing his new tweed jacket from Meakers of Piccadilly and sitting on a rock in the Lake District
portable Scrabble
record player with radio, AM-FM
flashlight
glass paperweight with pink fish inside—birthday

present from H when I was six or seven
asthma inhaler

and not much else besides clothes.

Is this everything I own? Kurt was surprised at my not having brought a copy of *Household* with my novel in it. He wanted to read it, and I was just as glad I couldn't lend it to him. Why did H have to tell everyone about it?

The Land Grant to Antonio Martinez,
Resident of the Kingdom of New Mexico

. . . On the inside of the Luceros' River . . . there is a valley in which the native say they cultivated and that they were never disturbed therein by the said Sergeant Major [first owner], and that they will abide by whatever may be given them by the said Antonio (grantee), whom I took by the hand and led over said tract of land, and he plucked up grass, cast stones, and shouted aloud, entering upon the Royal Possession which I gave him in the name of his Majesty.

(October 26, 1716)
Miguel Tenorio de Alba
Secretary of State and War

My land, described in the long, complicated Abstract of Title that Kurt turned over to me this afternoon. I have just read this passage for the first time, to find that H and the children and I went through an old ritual today without knowing it. We walked my boundaries with Kurt, and we plucked up grass, cast stones, and shouted aloud.

N and I should officially be joint owners, but Kurt has been kind enough to let me make a down payment and do things formally later, when N can sign papers with me. If anyone questions the arrangement, I am just the tenant. But really the house is mine.

Kurt stayed after the others had left, to show me how to light the stoves (very frightening. The kitchen one flares up.) and how to get water. There is a well in the front yard, though only four feet deep, and the water must be boiled for twenty minutes before it can be used. He left jugs that I can fill with drinking water at the laundromat, and in an emergency I could borrow from the Ortegas next door. They have all the modern conveniences, including a well two hundred feet deep.

Something unsettling: Kurt offered me a gun along with the dishes and paintings and everything else he was leaving—as if it were a household item I ought not to be without. He seemed uncomprehending when I refused.

When he had gone, I opened a can of soup and then found I couldn't light the stove. It was all right cold, but I was glad I wasn't serving it to N.

The sunset behind the big window was even grander than I had expected it to be. It made me feel as inarticulate as the hippies H tells me about, who stare at the scenery and say "Oh, wow!" and think they're being creative. She says she wants to shake them and say, "*You* didn't make that sunset; you're just the audience."

curtain material	bug spray (spiders)
dishes	broom
pans	hot plate?
cooking spoons	sleeping bag
towels	blanket

dish rack
chairs
hooks for hangers
Indian rug (price?)
chest of drawers

refrigerator (Around here, a desire for this is regarded with scorn, as if it were color television. H apologizes for hers.)
hat

I've never before thought of sunlight as something to hide from. Maybe the dime store would sell a sort of modified cowboy hat. I can't see myself in the pretty gondolier type H has, with yellow ribbons hanging down the back.

H has lent me, along with bedding, a batch of New Mexico books—Mabel Dodge Luhan, Brett, both Lawrences. They ought to make strange reading, interspersed with chapters of *Sense and Sensibility.* I always seem to be reading three or four books at once.

This room has a good atmosphere—enveloping and sturdy. Will be even better with curtains and a reading lamp.

Buy lamps.
candles
investigate about fireplace.
towel racks
mirror

I suspect the outhouse of spiders. And the door won't close all the way.

May 31

I should send N that beautiful passage from the Abstract of Title. He would never be able to resist language like that.

N is the only person I know who understands my captivation with words. Just words, all by themselves, apart from anything that can be done with them. Sometime during the first conversation we ever had, we discovered that both of us got abnormally angry at hearing words misused. "Do you know which one bothers me most?" I asked him.

" 'Disinterested?' 'Enormity?' "

"No, or 'noisesome' or 'decimated' or 'one-dimensional.' How can anything be one-dimensional?" I hesitated. I had never told this to anyone before. "It's 'raddled.' "

He just looked at me.

"People seem to think it means haggard or ravaged or something like that. Some dictionaries even think so."

"Doesn't it?"

"No. It just means rouged. Reddened. As with an old raddled hag. That's a word you never see except when it's used wrong."

"I don't believe I ever see it."

"I do, all the time. It's amazing. There was a description of a building the other day, an old raddled building. There's another meaning—a short stick or pole and therefore a wattle—but that has a different derivation, and neither of them has anything to do with deterioration. See the O.E.D." I could feel my own cheeks reddening because the subject of conversation was such an emotional one for me.

N looked at me in wonderment. "I believe you," he said.

It was raining when I woke up this morning, a gray New England drizzle which must have been going on for hours. The light in the room was dim and greenish, and the weeds outside leaned toward the big window and clung to it. A dismal sight. It hadn't occurred to me that it would ever rain here—except for those brief afternoon showers that yield nothing but rainbows and a freshness in the air.

What bothered me was finding that there is a leak in the roof—a fairly large one, to judge by the size of the puddle on the living-room floor. Kurt explained the roof to me before I moved in. Above the rough boards *(latias)* laid across the *vigas* is a solid layer of dirt at least a foot thick, and on top of that is tarpaper which looked fairly strong when I inspected it with him a few days ago. Was there a leak then? I've never had to think about roofs before, only ceilings.

I've discovered a new disadvantage of dirt floors; everything you put on them gets dirty. Of course; but I never had a reason to think about it till this morning when I picked up the shirt and jeans I had left beside the mattress last night. More matting might help, or some real linoleum.

I may have mastered the stove! You have to spin the handle under a burner, and then wait until air bubbles rise in the glass kerosene container and the wick becomes shiny. It lighted on my first try, and I was terribly proud. I hated to let it go out.

I could see that the racks for Kurt's canvases would have to come down before I could do anything else to the house. They took up more than half the space between head height and ceiling in both rooms, and when they were empty they looked like nothing but a dusty, unsafe jungle gym. I went to get help.

As I drove to H's house, the sky was solid gray with the mountains looming in dark gray masses against it.

A blue jeep was parked next to Seth's truck, and when H let me into the kitchen I saw Bronson McKinney sitting at the table and looking toward the door, with a quizzical expression all prepared on his face.

"Good morning," he said. "Aren't you up early." As if I had a reputation for sleeping late.

The only way to deal with Bronson, I have told myself, is to treat him as if he were a normal, well-meaning person. "Oh, good," I said, imitating a hearty gym teacher from my past. "Maybe you can help me. Do you know anything about roof leaks?"

"Don't tell me there's a hole in your roof," he said, stirring his coffee, "because I won't believe you."

"Why not?"

He just looked at me with a slight smile. "He's teasing you," H said. She was clearing dishes off the table and rinsing them at the sink.

"Would any sane person buy a house without inspecting the roof? You're imagining things. Go back and look again." He was still smiling, so no one could accuse him of being unpleasant. Also, he must have been genuinely glad to hear about the leak.

"Just a minute," H said. "I'll ask Seth what you should do." She ran outside toward the shed that Seth uses as a studio. She was gone before I had a chance to follow her in a way that would seem natural.

Bronson continued to look steadily at me with his drooping, colorless eyes. A piece of his hair hung over the side of his head, much longer than the rest. I couldn't help staring at it, trying mentally to fit it into place on the other side of the part and see if it was still too long. It looked as if it would be. "And what's wrong with you?" he asked me.

"You mean now? This morning? Nothing's wrong. Why?"

He looked disgusted, as if I were being deliberately simple. "No, I don't mean this morning. You came all the way to New Mexico. People never come here unless there's something wrong somewhere else."

"I came to visit my sister."

"Alone?"

"Yes." If he didn't have to explain anything, neither did I.

"You didn't just come to visit. You bought a house."

"True. I did that, I think, because it's the sort of thing I wouldn't expect myself to do." Trying to explain my motives to hostile strangers isn't characteristic of me either, but the thought came to me so suddenly that I expressed it without thinking about who it was I was talking to. I smiled belatedly, as if I had told a joke.

"Scandal, failure, bad lungs, bad marriage." He tapped long fingers on the table, counting off reasons. "Did you know that almost everyone who comes here turns out to have been divorced at some time? When they run away, this is where they run to."

"You too?" He wasn't the only one who could ask bold questions.

"I was born here. My mother came after her divorce. So what's *your* problem?"

H came in then, dripping rain. "Tar paper, Seth says, and you put it on with roof cement, preferably on a hot day. Get Kurt to help you."

"I'm surprised Seth has heard of roof cement," Bronson said. "It's a bad sign. A successful artist avoids knowing anything about house building. Tell him that." I was reminded of what H had said about Bronson's conflict between poetry and bathtubs. When I looked at his hands, I saw that the skin was worn and roughened, presumably by grout. He sounded bitter, but I am beginning to think he always does.

I arranged to borrow a ladder from H and went to the hardware store to buy a crowbar, hammer, and screwdriver, besides some of the items on the lists I made last night. Then I bought groceries. Scene at the First National: A dark-braided Indian woman in clumsy knee-high moccasins, accepting a sample of cottage cheese from a white-uniformed clerk. "This is Foremost cottage cheese," the demonstrator said, and the woman ate it without changing expression. I hoped she wouldn't buy any but am afraid she did. The Indians don't even bake their own bread anymore, H says.

My letter to N was gone from the mailbox when I came back. No mail for me, but at least the postman had been there. (Must replace Kurt's name with mine right away. Buy paint.) In the afternoon H drove over with the ladder and we tore down the painting racks. Luckily, Kurt had used as few nails as possible to put them up. The dust was terrible, and there were spider webs, some of them occupied. We managed by using a lot of bug spray and keeping our hands out of dark corners.

Angie Ortega came over to watch us, with a black-eyed baby in her arms and a little boy hiding behind her. She didn't entirely approve, I suspect. Luis is always doing things to improve their house, she says, but he never expects her to help except by keeping the children out of the way. "He has his pride," she said proudly.

"So has Seth," H said, and laughed. "He's so proud he won't even put up a screen door because it might set a precedent."

Although the house looks better without the racks, the walls have turned out to be even dirtier and more battered than I imagined. Someone long ago did put on several coats of whitewash, but the surface is scarred with mud-colored scratches and nail holes that leak loose sand and bits of straw. The base of the walls for at least a foot up from the floor is damp—not just under the leak but all the way around the room. Is this true only on rainy days? (No, I suspect.) I put it on my mental list of things to ask Kurt about before I went off to have dinner with H and Seth.

June 2

I never know how much of my self-doubt shows. Sometimes it seems hidden under a false arrogance, and sometimes even the children see it. Nora stood next to me today when I was talking to H, and leaned against my shoulder. "Nobody's perfect, Anne." She was trying to comfort me.

I looked as offended as I could. "Not even I?"

"Oh, Anne. You're such a funny aunt." Nora's ears stick out a bit, like mine, and the right one is pointed in the same way. The tubercle of Darwin, according to my father-in-law.

If I had to sum up Seth, I could: He knows the zip code of the MacDowell colony.

He does, too. He actually said it tonight when he was recommending that I apply to go there in the fall. "Just mention my name," he said, and then he reeled off the address without looking it up. I didn't dare to look at H. I have to be careful not to seem critical of Seth when she is there, must keep reminding myself of the rules: She is allowed to criticize him, but I am not even supposed to agree with her criticisms. It's hard to hide the indignation I feel when she tells me about something heartless he has done, and of course I can't always hide it—but I try at least to keep from making any general statements about him.

The truth is that, in spite of anything H says about Seth, she expects me to like him.

June 3

And there are other subjects that generate too much emotion between H and me. The trouble is that we think we understand each other.

"But I thought it was right, Elinor," said Marianne, "to be guided wholly by the opinion of other people. I thought our judgments were given to us merely to be subservient to those of our neighbors. This has always been your doctrine, I am sure." A catty remark from *Sense and Sensibility*. It is infuriating to have our ideas described by other people, because even when no sarcasm is intended (as of course it is in Marianne's statement, though I'm not sure the author admits it), other people are sure to get them wrong. In this case E doesn't react as I would, just corrects her sister calmly. I am not so calm.

We were in H's kitchen this morning, talking about Seth again. H had been searching for adjectives to describe his most unbearable qualities and had just decided that the closest she could come was "inhuman." Then, "I wonder if I married him because he's so much like you," she said dreamily, idly.

I just looked at her and wondered why she had said a thing like that. For the effect on me or for something to say to fill in a silence? Or because she thought it was true. I thought of Marianne and Elinor.

"That's a compliment, of course," H went on. "You're both so efficient about your work. So . . . I don't know."

"Ruthless?" N's word.

She looked pleased. "That's what I mean. You don't allow your personal lives to interfere, no matter what happens. I admire that."

I tried to be fair. "I suppose that must be the impression I give sometimes, but it isn't true. I wish it were."

"You remember when we used to go sketching," H said, "and I did all those messy watercolors, and the colors ran together and came out muddy and I painted so hard that the paper was wrinkled?"

"Not always. Some of your pictures were good."

"But too emotional. Not controlled, like yours. You didn't even take your paints with you."

"Yes, I did."

"You just drew those careful pencil sketches with little notes on the side about the colors, and then when you got home you filled in the outlines."

"You're thinking of that time at Brook Farm, when I forgot the paintbox."

"And the results were so much better than mine." H laughed. "I often think of you that way, practically painting by number."

If those are her memories, that's what they are, but I remember things too. "You used to sign all your pictures," I said.

"With a great big sloppy monogram I had invented, like Whistler's butterfly." She seemed to think of this as a session of fond reminiscences. "But you would never put anything but those neat initials, very tiny, in the corner. If you put anything at all. We haven't changed, I guess. You're so modest about your book, using your maiden name and not wanting people at the college to know about it. If I had written a whole book, I would tell everybody and get all the credit I could."

"It wasn't a whole book, and I don't think of it as credit. Responsibility is more like it. Nat and I just thought the English department people would be happier not knowing, so we didn't tell them, that's all. And then when they found out, they misinterpreted our not telling them."

"Really? It seems so like you, wanting to be anonymous."

"No. I don't know what is like me, but we really didn't do it for my sake. We just thought that if my real name was on the cover of the magazine, somebody we knew might see it on the rack in the A & P. We couldn't think of any other reason for any of them to read anything so lowbrow."

"Oh, but I thought it was good. Very well written." She paused, as if she hesitated to offend me. "The plot was a little sentimental, of course. That part where the sick baby reaches out his little arms and his callous mother suddenly sees how appealing he is."

"Yes, wasn't that awful? You can see why I didn't mind people's not knowing I'd written it. I was glad my picture didn't have to be in the front of the magazine, too, which is unfair, because when I'm reading a book, I always want to know what the author looks like."

"Oh, me too."

"But somebody did read it, as it turned out, and recognized the description of the ears on the statues at the entrance of the Administration Building and therefore assumed the whole story must be about the college. Then she started calling up her friends and telling them they were in it."

"You shouldn't have described the Administration Building," H said primly.

"I couldn't resist. But the worst part of the scandal must have been when everyone knew about the book but didn't know who had written it. Anne is such a common name, and I heard later that at least four people were suspected. Then someone had the idea of asking the departmental secretaries to look up the maiden names of all the wives named Anne. So I was unmasked before I even heard any of the rumors.

"What fun. I almost wish I had been there."

"I wish you had," I said.

June 3

I have been afraid lately that people at home might think I was running away from their reaction to my book, and I suppose that's what many of them must think. And it wasn't even that kind of book. Not at all.

But life doesn't offer many surprises in that college town where the sidewalks in winter are white-walled tunnels for four months and the air is too cold to breathe. The book gave them something to be excited about. Even I, at the still center of the storm, could sense the excitement that surrounded me—the women who cried over the telephone to each other and the men who spent hours of scholarly work tracing references and putting footnotes into their copies of *Household* magazine.

I was too well behaved before last fall; that was the trouble. I even went to their silly teas in a hat. If I had been like the mountain-climbing wife in the anthropology department, with her lederhosen and gray pony tail, they wouldn't have been so surprised. But I see now that they must have been under the impression that I was one of them. Maybe I had an obligation to make sure they knew from the beginning that I was an outsider, and a dangerous one. As it was, when they found out what I had done, they thought of me as a traitor.

On the other hand, when they had read the book (or only heard about it in most cases), they didn't understand me any better than they had before. Worse, in fact.

They didn't know, for instance, that I really could sympathize with them because of personal experience. My father used to refer to H and me in his sermons sometimes, so I know how it feels. None of us can escape from other people's ideas of us, but we don't usually have to know what those ideas are. (There was one Sunday afternoon when H cried for three hours because in talking about her in that morning's service Father had made a humorous reference to the way she monopolized the family bathroom.) And like my victims, we were usually less upset by the truth than by exaggeration or inaccuracy. "But I don't even *know*

Italian," I hear that one woman protested. She had just discovered a passage in my party scene where a character she suspected (wrongly) of being modeled on herself was trapped in a strained Italian conversation with the most urbane member of the Romance Languages department.

Some people on the campus even had parties just for the purpose of discussing my book. I wasn't invited, so I don't know any exact details, but my friends (I still had a few, even if not all of them chose to be seen with me in public.) told me enough. One man actually discussed the book with the students in his classes. He and his wife were both convinced (rightly) that he was the original of a particularly pompous character, and they told everyone. This surprised me, as I hadn't thought they realized he was like that or would want to admit it if they did.

One thing I learned last fall was to avoid people who started conversations by telling me how much they liked my style. Such people, I found, were only looking for an opportunity to tell me about all the things they didn't like. There was a woman who loved my style and said so at a party, adding, "Of course Reginald doesn't agree with me," and pulling Reginald by the elbow into our group. Reginald is a well-known authority on Pope and Swift. Six feet six, with eyes that look in two different directions, he pointed the front of his face at me and started to explain that I was not only malicious (which apparently was already a well-known fact) but frivolous. I could see his point about the frivolity but had to deny the malice. I couldn't tell whether he even heard what I was saying; his eyes were looking past me over both my shoulders, and he kept on talking about my cruelty. If he read this now, he could easily point out my mentioning his eyes as another example of spite, and yet they were what had the greatest effect on me, and while it might be tactful not to mention them, it wouldn't be truthful.

The oddest thing is that it was his wife, my admirer, who discovered the story in her copy of *Household* and called up her friends to tell them that they were characters in it. (She wasn't one herself.) Without her, perhaps no one there would have known, and I'm sure that all of us would be happier today.

June 4

Frivolity, yes. The *Household* novel started out as a joke, with neither of us having the slightest notion of its really being published. Which was why I wasn't more careful.

We first got the idea at a party one night in Indiana when I was explaining my job to some people who found it fascinating. I worked at that time for Dr. Raymond Peck, a psychology professor who moonlighted by doing readership surveys for *Household*. My job was to read the short novel in the back of each month's issue, write a summary for Dr. Peck, and then go over the transcripts of telephone interviews conducted with typical readers who were asked to give their reactions to the novel. I graded the interviews on a scale ranging from −80 ("depressing," "tiresome," "far-fetched," "fantastic and poor") to +80 ("marvelous," "It was so wonderful I told my husband about it," etc.) and then calculated the mean score for that story. (Anything over +50 was pretty good.) I also picked out some of the pithiest reader comments, to be quoted in our official report on the story. That report was always written by Miss Mallard, Dr. Peck's secretary, in a tone that patronized the story as well as the poor fools who were ignorant enough to enjoy it. "Reward factors," "anxiety," "personal involvement," and "strongly negative factors" were some of her favorite terms.

Not a very satisfying job for me in any way, but we needed the money. It didn't occur to me at the time that I was picking up information I would ever be able to use. But then when we were at that party and I was describing the Peck-Mallard system and telling what elements a story had to have if it was to earn at least a +70 reward score, someone said, "Why don't you write one?" and I realized that I probably could. So we all started to work on it right away, with everyone putting in suggestions, and eventually we worked out a plot and characters, and I took notes. It was a good party game. Everyone said so, and then we all went home.

A few years later, when we had moved to New York State and I didn't have a job yet, we still needed money. "Did you save those notes for the *Household* novel?" N asked me one day. He had been thinking he might be able to do something with them, he said. He read through the notes and seemed excited, and I think he even wrote a few pages of dialogue before realizing that all he was doing was rather ingeniously postponing his work on Dickens. "I'm sorry," he said to me, "but I'm afraid you'll have to write the thing." That was how I turned out to be the one who wrote the book.

It was odd. I had never in my life written anything I wasn't assigned to write except for letters and family birthday verses and such things. Writing had never been hard for me, but even for school assignments I had always chosen to write essays rather than stories, and I doubted quite strongly that I was qualified to write a *Household* novel. My style, I thought, would be mechanical, and our formula would show, and any editor who looked at the story would be able to tell that it hadn't been written with any conviction at all.

As soon as I started to write, my cynical attitude disappeared. I found I was getting interested in the characters and what happened to them. The college doctor's wife, for instance, whom we had cast as our troublemaker. We had made her a former model, married to the doctor when he still had dreams of becoming a fashionable neurologist. No wonder she was restless, I began to think as I wrote the quarrel scene that opened the story, and after a while I was seeing her as Emma Bovary. The same sort of thing happened with the other characters. Although I knew they were unreal and sometimes asinine, I couldn't help becoming involved in their problems. I'm not saying that the story was anything but trash, but the point is that I discovered I had a real talent for producing trash. "She flowed into his arms and melted there," I actually found myself writing, feeling the thrill of creation. It was quite difficult for me later to force myself to cut out the whole sentence.

N never came to take the story seriously, though, nor to understand how it felt to be writing it. "You've got to put in more clichés," he would command after reading through a random page. "I can't!" I remember protesting. "I mean, I'm bound to put in plenty of them, but not on purpose." In the end, in spite of spells of misplaced artistic integrity that made me want to preserve the most unnecessary parts of the story, I eliminated most of my easy phrases and made the whole thing as good as I could. As H said, it was well written.

June 4

I suppose I can understand why H told everyone here about the *Household* story. It was to give me credentials with her friends, as much for my sake as for hers. I have to make up for being a teacher's wife by being some kind of artist. But it's embarrassing, trying to explain without sounding as if I were just being modest, and people do keep asking questions.

"Why was everyone so angry?" Kurt asked me today when we were up on the roof fixing the leak.

"Because," I said, "I put real people in imaginary beds," and wished I hadn't said it. His blank, polite face showed that he didn't get the reference, and now I might have to explain that. And had it been wise to mention beds? Besides, what I had said wasn't true; the book didn't deal much with that sort of thing at all. *Household* hadn't heard yet about the New Freedom, and even if it had, I wouldn't have been able to imagine people in N's department sleeping with each other. Not even with the people they were married to, most of them, though all the little quarrels and betrayals were easy enough.

Kurt has the kind of overexpressive face that places a burden on the other people in a conversation. Large, benevolent features and about five versatile wrinkles in his forehead. I find myself trying to say things to justify the interest he shows, and I never feel I've succeeded. "You mustn't respect me too much," I said then, trying to change his expression before it made me say something really unkind. "Do you know how many hours of my life I have spent with a perfectly empty mind, just scraping old paint off radiators?"

"You've worked hard, Anna," he said. "Can't I respect that?"

I gave up. "If you want to." I'm afraid I take Kurt's good will for granted by now.

The view from the roof was beautiful today, as always. Mountains, sky, the soft green tops of trees, and two horses running in a field. But the sun was hitting the back of my head, and the landscape was overpowering. I wondered what I was doing here. But I knew I ought to say something nice to Kurt. "Thank you for helping me fix this." I pointed to the square of tarpaper we had just put on. "I was afraid of what Nat would think."

"When is he coming?" Kurt asked.

"I don't know." I went first down the ladder.

"Did Nat mind about your book?" We sat at the table, waiting for the water to boil for tea.

"It's very complicated. He was pleased when it was first accepted. Then he was worried about people's feelings, so we decided not to tell anyone. Then when they found out and it turned out that he was right to worry, he was angry with them. Some of the full professors were very vindictive. Nat was suddenly scheduled for five eight o'clocks, for instance, and he was put on a committee that meets all the time and never does anything. The thing is, some of them thought *he* had really written the book."

"Why?" Kurt's eyebrows flew up, and the wrinkles appeared.

"One scene was set in a men's room, so they assumed

that only a man could have written it." It sounded as silly as ever. "I didn't describe the plumbing or anything. And there were other things—conversations in departmental meetings or in the President's office, where people knew I hadn't been, so they said Nat must have written the book himself or else taken notes for me."

"Didn't they know anything about how books are written?"

"No. Most people don't, I suppose, but we had thought that they would. They were almost all either English teachers or librarians. It was hard for Nat, but he never took it out on me."

Kurt looked disappointed. "So he was on your side all the way through."

"I don't think he ever actually wished I hadn't written it. Some of his colleagues even made a point of being especially kind to him, just to show how fair they could be. Then after a while the wrong people began to praise the book, for their own reasons. I hated that, but Nat liked it."

"What kind of people?"

"Dissatisfied students or teachers. People who wanted to take power away from people who had it. A teaching assistant came up to me at the departmental picnic with his glasses gleaming and said, 'I hear you've written an attack on the college. Right on!' He couldn't have read the story. It's surprising how many people talk about things they haven't read. I never realized it before. It was embarrassing. I was even invited to speak at meetings."

N knows quite well that what I wrote wasn't anti-administration propaganda, but he has begun, lately, to think that perhaps that's what I ought to be writing. He sees how trivial my work would appear to his fellow dissidents if they ever looked carefully at it, and he is uncomfortable. Why couldn't I change my habits and write about something important? he asked me not long ago. Why shouldn't I write about the SDS?

Impossible, I told him. Even if I could bring myself to write about them, what I wrote would turn out in the end to be a satire, just as the *Household* story had. "It would be much better from your point of view," I said, "if I joined the Young Americans for Freedom."

He refused to understand. "You could write a sympathetic description of our group if you tried."

"And it would have about as much life as one of those Russian murals of farm workers and glorious tractors." (Actually, I wasn't honestly sure that I could. He wouldn't see that I wasn't all that sympathetic.)

It was my starting the second story that made N completely exasperated with me. If, after managing to sell the first one, I had dismissed the whole business as an odd episode in our past and had concentrated on my library job, it would have been all right with him, and he probably wouldn't have gotten ideas about what I ought to be doing instead. But when the editors asked if I were working on anything else, I began to have pretensions, and I told them I might have something to show them soon. Also, once you write one story, you begin to see possibilities for others; you can't help it. Unfortunately, however, the story material I picked up from daily life was no more earth-shattering than anything we had put into the first novel. Although daily life was getting more serious all the time, my attitude toward it didn't seem to be.

There was one morning when N forgot his briefcase

and came back for it after I had spread out my papers all over the table. He didn't usually interfere with my writing, but I suppose he was pleased to see a newspaper clipping lying there on the corner of the table. He must have thought I was finally making use of a Current Event. Until he picked it up and saw what it was, and then he couldn't keep himself from reading it out loud. It was from the Fashion Queries column: " 'My daughter is being married in September at an afternoon ceremony. I am wearing an aqua coat and dress ensemble with shoes to match, and white gloves. Have an aqua whimsy which I hate. Would a white hat be appropriate? MRS. H.G.'

"Is that the kind of thing you think is important?" he asked me. "When you pick up the morning paper and you see by the headlines that 223 American soldiers died in Vietnam last week, what do you do? Turn to the Women's Page and clip out a piece of drivel like that. Don't you live in the world, like the rest of us?"

"But that's why." I don't know why I always try to explain to him. "Terrible things happen, but what really worries people most are the little things, the personal ones. How they appear to other people, whether they said something stupid last night." I knew I mustn't mention his difficulties with his mustache.

"Nonsense. I mean bullshit." He folded his arms and planted his feet apart in the new way that I mustn't mention either.

"All right, I have a trivial mind, but I did think it was interesting. This perfectly conventional woman, wanting to wear the right thing at her daughter's wedding so desperately that she writes to a fashion columnist, and yet she has a whimsy that she hates. All that emotion."

"What's a whimsy?" He couldn't resist asking.

"I don't know." I was tired of these conversations. "Something you wear on your head. It must be. But what interests me is why she hates it. Does it catch in her hair? Can't she drape it right? Does she feel like a fool in it? Will she throw it to the floor and stamp on it? Is it really the whimsy she hates? Or does it stand for something else that most people would consider more worth hating?"

He made a disgusted sound, the rage coming up through his nose. "Crime in the streets, no doubt. Were you going to write a story about *that?*" He looked at the clipping.

"I don't know. Not now. I don't care much for whimsy myself." I folded the piece of paper up small and dropped it into the wastebasket, making sure he saw. You have to pick up points where you can.

When he had left, I opened the newspaper and saw a whole page devoted to testimonials for something called Mitchum Anti-perspirant. A woman flung her hands into the air to expose dry armpits. "What a joy!" she was saying about her luxurious underarm dryness. On the opposite page a column on physical fitness began: "Today's exercise is in answer to the numerous inquiries for inner thigh help."

Somebody must care about these things.

June 6

Talking to Kurt about N made me remember N more realistically. I had been starting to romanticize him again, and that's dangerous—makes me write sentimental letters to someone who doesn't exist any more. "Socialistic, anarchistic syndicalism." For a minute after N had said it, I thought it was something he was against. "We must treat America as if it were an occupied country." One of the last things I heard him say. Nearly all of our recent quarrels have been about my work. N wants me to be socially useful. He would love it if I were a psychiatric social worker, for instance. "Is a hack writer what you really want to be?" he asks, and I can't help suspecting that it is.

June 7

But it isn't only that the things I choose to write about are frivolous. By N's standards now, my point of view and even my language are too ladylike altogether. How could it be otherwise? He knows the kind of background I come from (not so different from his own, but at least he had the benefit of the Army and of being a boy).

My mother grew up thinking that the worst word in the language was "ain't." (She used it to taunt her own mother when she felt devilish, shouting it and running out of the house and slamming the door.) It's possible that she still thinks so. Is it surprising that I can't identify with the people in Saul Bellow or Philip Roth? I read their books in wonder, amazed at the vulgarity and strangeness of the family life they write about. Whereas whenever I read Jane Austen, I see people I know. Am I the only one who feels this? Sometimes I think so. A woman at a party once told me, quite sincerely, how much she empathized with Herzog. To me he can't be anything but a character I don't understand and suspect to be masquerading as a professor; but when I read about Elinor Dashwood or Jane Fairfax, I recognize myself.

Dirty words. The code of the secret society that men belong to. The vocabulary of war and business and the rest of the real world. Of men impatient for women to leave so they can talk freely. This is the way it used to be. Now young girls use the same words and do it naturally, as far as I can tell. Good for them. But it's too late for me. I never even knew some of those words existed until recently, when they started appearing in print. And I had never heard them spoken aloud until N decided, not long ago, that he needed a more manly vocabulary. He claims to think I would talk that way too if I didn't restrain myself out of some hypocritical wish to be genteel. "You might at least say 'damn' occasionally," he says, but if I do, he says I sound insincere.

N used to be so different. I remember our first dinner together, when we found that we had both gone through the same bound sets of Dickens and Mark Twain when we were children—green and gold for Mark Twain, maroon for Dickens, with small print on thin paper. Neither of us had ever found anyone else who had read *Those Extraordinary Twins* at the back of *Pudd'nhead Wilson,* as well as *Hard Times* and *Roughing It,* and we had met almost nobody who understood if we mentioned Mrs. Nickleby or the gentleman in small-clothes who courted her with vegetable marrows. It seemed as if we had been waiting all our lives to meet each other.

June 11

Kurt knows a Spanish woman who will build my fireplace. She must belong to a different social class from Angela Ortega. Kurt is kind about helping with plans for the house, isn't going to abandon me after all, as I feared on the day it rained. (It rains every day now, a wild storm at one o'clock that lasts ten minutes and leaves a wonderful smell and brilliant light afterwards. Not like the dreary rain that one day.)

To make a genuine adobe floor, you mix dirt, sand, and straw with water and pack it down. Then you kill an ox and let the blood soak into the floor. (Or use linseed oil if you're squeamish.) After it dries, this is supposed to give a nice shiny finish.

Flagstones have more appeal to me, I think. We can get beautiful red ones from a man named Velasquez. I had to stop myself from agreeing too quickly just because of the man's name. I haven't even seen the stones yet, simply take the word of K and H. Still, I suppose I'll buy them.

I overuse the word "beautiful" now. I can't help it.

Hollyhocks. I never liked them before. They always looked coarse and artificial to me—made of crepe paper, with too much fuzzy pollen in the middle. Suddenly, here, I understand what they're for. Gaudy colors and rough textures seem right. I love to feel my tastes changing and expanding. (Effect of the altitude? But it's true.)

June 12

I tried out H's early Bronson McKinney bathtub today, while the children pounded along the corridor outside and screeched at each other in what appeared to be French. (*"Traîtresse. Sale cochon,"* I swear I heard Tomas yelling.) School is out for the summer, and they don't have much to do but fight. The two girls, when they aren't reading or braiding colored ribbons into each other's hair, work on self-assigned tasks that remind me of the things H and I did as children. Melisande seems to have the same fanatical dedication to her projects that I remember in H, and the same rage when she is disturbed. Nora is her cheerful slave, but Tomas is too young to stay interested in anything for very long, and he has his own rages. Lately they've been building an elaborate, nerve-wracking mobile which so far refuses to balance. It's made from coat hangers and origami birds and will probably be lovely if Melisande doesn't fall into despair and destroy it before it's finished.

The bathtub is not a complete success. It has a blue tile surface and is made in two levels so that the bather theoretically can sit on the upper one with his feet in the well below and relax in hot water up to his chin. It should be luxurious, but Bronson built it before finding out that the capacity of a bathtub mustn't be much larger than that of the water heater. The well at the lower end of the tub can just be filled before the water begins to run cold, and there is a choice between a big cool bath and a little warm one. I tried the warm bath today, but I'm too tall to crouch in the well, and my shoulders were cold. Next time I'll take H's advice and settle for a shower. ("No architect can build any house well who does not know something of anatomy." A quote from Vitruvius that I found in my copy of Emerson when I got home.)

When I came out of the bathroom, there was a smell of turpentine. Kurt was in the kitchen, working on his painting of Gretchen and H. It shows them sitting at a table set with a coffee pot and cups and a loaf of blue and orange French bread. Gretchen leans her cheek mournfully on one hand while H smiles and holds a cup at an angle chosen by Kurt to show off the curve of her wrist. H was posing with her cup when I came out, but it was Bronson she was talking to, not Gretchen.

"Hi, how was the bath?" she said, being playful. She had never complained about the bathtub to Bronson, she admits.

"Fine." I stood behind Kurt and examined the picture. I was surprised. "But you've given Harriet blue eyes," I said.

Kurt smiled vaguely, standing back from H to observe her position. "That's right."

The eyes were a luminous violet-blue, exactly the color Kurt would think was appropriate for H. "Why?" I couldn't help myself.

Bronson gave the sardonic, classifying laugh I might have expected. "Why not?"

Because, I thought, Harriet's eyes are the most extraordinary thing about her, and if Kurt gets the color wrong it shows that he doesn't want to know what she is really like; he hasn't looked at her real eyes. He would leave out the worn look on H's face, I knew, but would use the slight sag of her shoulders because it was graceful. But there seemed no point in offending Kurt or trying to make him into a different kind of painter. "Because they're not blue. Because they're a beautiful hazel color," I said. "I'm literal. You ought to know that by now."

Later, when Kurt and Bronson had driven off with Seth in the truck, H said, "There's something about really overbearing men." I wasn't sure which of them she was talking about. Not Kurt, anyway. "You remember how we used to be in love with Mr. Darcy and Sherlock Holmes."

"And Mr. Rochester. I used to think of him every time I tried to play the piano. Jane Eyre told him she only played a little and he made her play for him anyway until he found out she was telling the truth, and then he made her stop. I always thought that was exactly what would have happened to me. But I've never been attracted to men like that in real life. Only nice ones. Not weak, I mean, but human." But I was afraid H would think I wanted to discuss N, and I changed the subject.

June 16

I had never written anything about N before I began this journal. It wasn't a matter of principle, although I think (still) that it would be wrong to use even part of him in a fictional character; it was because we were so close to each other that I never saw him as someone to be explored and conjectured about. If you know too much about anyone, you don't know where to start. But now that I am away from him, scenes come into my mind, most of them based loosely on reality, and N, in a strange, exaggerated form, is in every one of them.

For instance:

She was sitting at her desk, crossing out most of what she had written the day before. Too many adjectives and qualifications. And why did the wife of that philosophy professor last night at dinner have to turn out to be hard of hearing, right after A had invented a rather pathetic faculty wife with a new hearing aid that she hadn't learned to control yet? A's character was history department, but it wasn't enough of a disguise. And who would believe she was based on one of A's father's parishioners long ago, a kindly woman who wore her hair puffed out on one side in an attempt to hide the cord and who spent a large part of every trustees' meeting groping in her bosom, trying to adjust the instrument that was giving out distracting squeals? The philosopher's wife had a more efficient hearing aid and wasn't like A's character in any other way, but it wouldn't make any difference. This was almost as bad as the time A had finally given her heroine a name and then met someone with the same name (first *and* last) the next day. But the change then had been easier to make.

She heard their car rumble into the driveway, then N's boots on the stairs. "Damn," she said conscientiously.

He came into the room breathing hard and flourishing a stack of yellow paper. "Good. You're not busy. This has to be typed up pronto." He handed her the papers.

"Pronto?" N's vocabulary was becoming rich and strange.

"Right." He sat heavily on the studio couch, flung his boots into a corner, and lay down, closing his eyes. "It's our manifesto." He was massaging his eyebrows. "Mary Beth wrote it up."

"I see." A hadn't accomplished much today anyway, but how could he know that? Mary Beth's handwriting was the half-printed kind, with circles for the dots over the *i*'s. Her spelling was bad, but A stopped herself from saying so. "Do you want to keep all these exclamation points?" she couldn't help asking.

"If you think they belong. Use your judgment!" He had always hated exclamation points, and he knew that she knew it.

"I'll cut out the triple ones." She put a stencil into the typewriter and made two mistakes as soon as she began to type. "You say she's a graduate student? In *English?*" She picked up a razor blade and scraped the stencil, trying to imagine Mary Beth's face.

"Yes. What's wrong?" His eyes were still closed.

"Then she ought to know that 'phenomena' is plural."

"Of course she does. It's just a slip, obviously."

" '*This* phenomena *is*'?"

He took a deep breath. "Change the grammar if you object to it. What matters is to get this typed and distributed."

"I suppose she thinks 'media' is singular too." But she kept on typing, feeling angry with N and Mary Beth for making her into a shrew.

N sat up and thumped his feet to the floor. "I haven't asked her. Shall I ask her? Shall I tell her you want to know? That it's important to you?"

Mary Beth's mistakes were exactly the kind that, as recently as last year, N had been accustomed to read to A, in amusement and exasperation, from student themes, but she couldn't pretend to herself that she had thought he would be amused now to hear her point them out. Aside from an evident personal involvement in the document she was typing, he had begun lately to change his ideas about the importance of grammar or even of logic.

He walked heavily to the kitchen, and A could hear him fumbling with cupboard doors. After three years in the same apartment, he still didn't know where anything was kept. He came back with a large glass of milk and began to drink it slowly, holding the glass with both hands and looking into it as if each sip of milk gave him just strength enough to take the next one.

All right, he was tired, but she knew that already. It wasn't fair for him to ask for so much sympathy. Wasn't it enough that she was typing his absurd manifesto?

"Why do they say 'liberate' when what they mean is 'capture'?" she asked, and waited for him to throw the glass at her.

He never threw things. "Have you finished with it?" he asked. "Mary Beth's waiting to run it off in the English office. Three hours of sleep last night, meetings all day, and she's ready for more work. She's a wonder, that girl. Never stops smiling in spite of everything." He took the papers from A, sighed deeply a few times to store up oxygen for the evening, and ran away down the stairs.

A hadn't met MB then and didn't know why she had such a definite mental image of her—a big blond girl with a flushed face and restless hands. The type who, in A's day, would have owned fifteen cashmere sweaters (probably still did but maybe didn't wear them because of being a revolutionary). "I HATE MARY BETH," A typed on a clean piece of paper, then realized that she didn't even know the girl's last name. Well, it wasn't necessary. She added "MARY BETH IS A FASCIST PIG," then tore the paper into very thin strips, rolled them up and put them under an empty cereal box in the kitchen wastebasket, covered the typewriter, sat down in front of her notebook, and got back to work. Her faculty wife character had to be deaf because of the scene later when the children thought she couldn't hear them. A could take out unfortunate resemblances later if she had to.

How inaccurate I can be when I write in the third person. I did type that manifesto, but not because N asked me to, exactly. He came in with it—five scribbled yellow pages he didn't quite know what to do with. "Our 'manifesto,'" he said in humorous quotes. "Two days of arguments, and all we can come up with is this. Minor revolutions do not produce great literature." He handed it to me. "Not even great sentences." He slumped onto the couch and yawned. "Or great phrases."

The pages were hard to read. Portions of the text were crossed out or added in three different colors of ink, and the edges looked as if they had been chewed by a hamster. "Would you like me to type it?" I offered. It was clear that somebody would have to.

"Oh, no. Not if you're busy." But he looked so relieved that of course I got out the typewriter immediately.

"I see what you mean," I said after I finished the first sentence. I was trying to revise as I typed, but after a while I gave up and hardly changed anything. The text was crammed with abstract words like "fascism," "imperialist," and "justice," and it mentioned a great many variegated grievances. "They've tried to put an awful lot into it, haven't they?" I said, feeling a jolly rapport with N.

"You can say that again." He was lying back with his eyes closed.

I got reckless after struggling with a particularly cluttered paragraph which had thirteen separate arrowed additions converging on it from the margins. "Wow," I said. "They've mentioned 'the People' eight times so far. Just like the Bill of Rights."

"I didn't count." His tone was cool, but I didn't notice at the time.

"But the effect is different somehow," I said. "You were right. It lacks beauty." He didn't say anything, and I went on to the next page. "At least they don't say 'so-called,'" I said after a while. "That's a right-wing word."

He sat up. "Look. It's nice of you to do this for me, but I wish you'd stop criticizing. This document is an example of *nobody's* style; you know that. Mary Beth managed to put it together from what twenty people were shouting at her all at once, and I think it's a miracle if it makes any sense at all."

I was ashamed. The tone of the paper was arrogant, but the intent wasn't bad, and many of the charges were true: Some of the professors at the college were inaccessible to the students, and a few of them did have Government contracts to do secret and probably immoral things, and the macaroni in the cafeteria did taste like slippery dishrags.

"Mary Beth is a decent, intelligent girl," N said. "She doesn't have much imagination, but she's conscientious. She wrote a B+ term paper for me last semester."

I was childishly pleased to hear that he hadn't given her an A. "I'm sorry," I said. I finished typing the manifesto and gave it to N. I wished he could get more sleep; he looked so tired.

About a week later, Mary Beth came to our apartment. I didn't know N was expecting her till that afternoon when I saw him looking around the living room and rearranging the magazines. "Mary Beth is coming over tonight to help plan our strategy," he said, and I suspected then that his slightly dissatisfied expression meant that our apartment was too bourgeois and he didn't know what to do about it. He wasn't sure what I would think of MB either.

I hadn't been too far wrong in visualizing her, it turned out. She was a big, wholesome girl in purple paisley bell-bottom slacks, a beige cashmere sweater, and a red armband. No bra. I was disappointed to see that her brown hair was short, proving her to be less conventional than I would have preferred her to be. She twisted a strand of it round and round during the conversation that evening, and occasionally tried to bring it down to her mouth; maybe she had just had it cut. While she didn't look exactly like the debutante I had pictured, the expression on her face was right—blind ferocity when she talked about the Government or the college Administration (the Establishment) and blind adoration when she looked at my husband.

When we were introduced, she smiled at me in a friendly way that put me to shame. Her admiration of N was clearly large enough to include anyone who might turn out to be his wife.

"Were you a Girl Scout?" I asked her abruptly, and N looked at me as if I had gone mad.

"Yes." She looked surprised. "I got all the merit badges."

"Oh. I see." Something about her made me see her

in a green uniform, with the neckerchief and knee socks and everything. She bore a resemblance to one of the girls in my mother's troop, that was all, but the impression was very strong. Well, it made sense. Girl Scouts to SDA; some people just like to do things in groups.

"Annie, bring us some beer, will you?" N shouted when they had settled down on the floor with their notes. He never calls me Annie.

I went to the kitchen and got two bottles of beer, two glasses, and an opener and put them on a tray. N stared at the glasses, not knowing whether to call attention to them by asking me what they were for. He compromised by taking the bottles from the tray and shoving it under the couch. I saw him reach for the opener a little while later.

I didn't know whether to leave while they were conferring, and it was awkward. When MB had gone, I made some remark that let N know what I thought of her.

" 'Playing,' " he said, quoting me. "Do you know that Mary Beth's brother is in jail for refusing induction? How can you say she's just playing?"

Of course I hadn't known it. How could I?

Note: This scene is nearly all imagined, and in some basic way it is untrue. I have misrepresented N again, and myself as well.

June 17

N, coming in from a meeting I had told him I was not going to attend: "Well, where were you?"

I just looked at him. I couldn't even pretend to be

working. There was a new novel open on my lap—a comic one at that.

"I know how tiring these meetings are," he said. "I should know if anybody does. And sometimes they don't seem to be accomplishing anything. . . ." But that was admitting too much about the evening. He glared at me. "Have you written to Washington at least?"

I was reluctant to admit that I had. "Not because you told me to. Don't you see I have to choose which things to try to do something about?"

"I don't see it at all. Either you're concerned or you aren't."

"And that *everybody* has to choose? If you spend your life going to meetings, it's because that's the way you must spend it—the only way that's satisfying to you—not necessarily because you can accomplish anything by going to them."

The actual conversation wasn't like that at all. There was more emotion and repetition, and neither of us was so articulate. But N thinks I am in control of everything I say, and that's the way I appear when I try to recreate any of my dialogues with him. Reason is too important to me (Is that the fault of Jane Austen or the Unitarians?), and N has decided recently that he wants to live a life based on instinct. All right, I can see why; he was brought up in a scientific family, with scientific rules. But the rules are different now, and strong emotions, whether or not they have any depth or spontaneity, have suddenly become obligatory. This is his chance to let go and be socially approved at the same time. I've never known anybody more anxious than N to do the correct thing. He's the only man I know who really enjoyed—he doesn't want anyone to know this now—being in the Army, because he likes following orders. (None of this is true either, and all of it is true.)

I think it was rather good of me not to laugh at N's mustache problems. He had trouble getting it to hang down equally on both sides, and he was terrified that it would turn out to be bushy. He used to spend hours working on it with the nail scissors, asking my advice every few minutes, before he finally got it right.

June 18

Why do I distort N so when I write about him? The truth is that he doesn't even have a mustache.

" 'Extremism in the pursuit of liberty is no vice,' " I said to him that time after Mary Beth had left, agreeing, I thought, with him in his rejection of her bright idea of setting fire to the college president's desk with napalm. But he recognized neither the irony nor the quotation, just looked at me with surprised approval and wrote something in his notebook.

"As Senator Goldwater put it," I was forced to say, to prevent his using the quotation in public. I am kinder than he gives me credit for being.

He wasn't grateful.

There. That was true.

June 19

N wishes I were like my friend Ruth. She is one of those dark, delicate-looking women you see in the eastern part of the country, often behind the wheel of a large, bus-shaped vehicle covered with peace stickers and filled with children. (She has six.) Ruth spends hours each day driving her shabby blue van on short trips, and the SANE calendar on her kitchen bulletin board is filled with appointments in her neat handwriting: 9:00: David, dentist; 10:00: picket draft board (bring signs) ; 3:45: Kelly, music lesson. Clothes from cleaners, meat sale at Star, etc. She has her hair done once in a while (owns a wig for emergencies) and wears big round glasses that make her face look small and helpless. She never has time to stop and talk when she sees a friend, and she doesn't call on anyone unless she's carrying a petition. "Excuse me," she said to me once when I was talking to her on the telephone. "My other phone is ringing."

I can't describe people like Ruth without seeming to be against them, and yet really I'm not. Not at all. It's just that by herself, looked at individually, Ruth is so pathetic. She is so small, and she is trying to do so much. (I must be influenced by those glasses. She is obviously much stronger—physically and probably emotionally—than, for instance, I am.) And there is so little for her to enjoy. The time I've seen her look happiest was when she heard an announcement that a local supermarket had agreed to stop selling California grapes. She took guitar lessons a few years ago ("So she can sing protest songs?" N asked. It was before he had joined her world.) but gave up because she enjoyed them so much that she was afraid she must be wasting time. But then, she comes from Boston, where the biggest parties are benefits.

* * *

Elise was the opposite. A cellist just beginning to get professional engagements, married to a professor who was involved in politics. She came home one night toward the end of a meeting that N and I went to at their house. People were sitting all over the floor looking at maps and being assigned areas to canvass, when Elise came in, nodded briefly, propped her cello in the corner, and made her way between us to the kitchen to get a late supper. Her husband just glanced up as she went through, and she didn't join us again. She had been at a rehearsal. I wonder now whether there was any conflict over her lack of involvement in her husband's causes. They have moved to Stanford now, and probably I'll never know. I wish I had known her better. Of course, music is different from writing. It's harder to be political with a cello.

June 19, 1969

Dear Nat—

I think of you often, but I'm not sure it's really you. Are you planning to travel in this direction any time soon?

Love,
A.

The house is beautiful.

June 20

This morning I found a note I had written to N lying in the weeds near my mailbox. It was torn up into little pieces. I had the feeling people are said to have when they find that their houses have been broken into. My privacy had been violated, and my relationship to N, by someone who wished us ill. I wondered if children had done it out of mischief, or if the people in the neighborhood resent me. It was a very small thing to happen, and yet I was quite shaken.

Kurt made me feel better when I told him about it. Mailbox thieves aren't uncommon here, it seems, and it was probably just somebody looking for money. He was shocked to learn that I had put anything important into the mailbox. "You shouldn't leave your letters lying around like that," he said, and he suggested I rent a box in the Post Office.

"Don't they know that tampering with the mails is a federal offense?" I couldn't help asking. I suppose I deserved the tolerant look he gave me.

Oddly enough, the whole episode makes me more hopeful than before. The letter this morning may not be the only one that was destroyed. N may even have written to me. I get some mail, but who knows what else may have been in the box? I searched the weeds again later, but there was nothing.

Kurt is painting my portrait. That is, he is putting me into the picture he has already painted of H and Gretchen. There was too much empty space in the middle, he says, and he needed another figure to bring the two halves together. He worked on it today in H's kitchen, amid all sorts of activity that didn't seem to bother him at all. H was making gingerbread, and Seth was hammering in his studio. The children and some of their friends shuffled around the yard, howling rhythmically while Melisande beat time on the top of an oatmeal box. After a while Seth came out and shouted at H. "Harriet, can't you keep those kids quiet?" He wouldn't reprimand them himself, just kept telling H to do it. Their performance, she told me, was an imitation of the Easter fertility dance at the pueblo, and very accurate.

"I hope it doesn't work," I said, and was surprised at the way she looked at me. I had only meant to lighten the atmosphere.

Kurt worked on, oblivious. He paced around, squinting at me and grunting occasionally or murmuring "Anna." I looked up each time he did this until I realized that he was addressing not me but the picture he meant to paint. It is odd being called "Anna"—makes me feel my cheekbones widening and my eyes slanting wickedly. I concentrated on holding my head in the right position and examining the row of dried wishbones in front of the geraniums on H's windowsill.

H is trying to teach the children French. "*Doucement*," she called when she wanted them to quiet down. It's their secret language, to protect them from the children who speak Spanish in front of them at school. She has bought language records and plays them at the children's bedtime. I don't think I would ever have thought of doing a thing like that.

The painting was nearly finished when Kurt stopped working on it today. H, with intense blue eyes, gestures with her coffee cup at somber Gretchen while I float between them, cool, detached, observing. Or maybe that's only the way I see it. Someone who didn't know I was an afterthought might see me as fitting into the picture better. Kurt's idea of me is close to the way I imagined it. He has made my eyes larger than they really are, and my hair longer.

Kurt had promised to take me to the pueblo to see about getting some straw for mud-plastering. He was cleaning his brushes and putting away his tubes of paint when I saw Bronson's jeep stop in front of the house.

"Sister Anne in person," Bronson said to me as he came in. He dumped a newspaper on the table, and I recognized last Sunday's *Times*. It doesn't get here till at least Thursday. "News from the outside world."

"More student riots just for you, Anne," H said brightly, and then drew in her breath as she noticed a picture on the front page. "Doesn't that look like Nat?" She held up the paper.

"No," I said automatically as the others looked at me. The man in the picture was in the center of a group of milling students. His mouth was open and his face distorted, and it was hard to tell what he looked like. Still, the shape of his sideburns was familiar, and that could be N's blue work shirt. The picture had been taken at N's college. "I don't think so," I said.

H studied the picture. "I don't see how it could be, actually. I can't imagine Nat yelling in public. Still, it does look like him."

I went off to the pueblo with K, leaving H and Bronson to think what they liked.

But I think it was N in the picture. When Kurt and I got back with two huge bundles of straw, H gave me the news section of the paper. Seth never reads it, she said, and she was through with it. I think she knew I might want to keep it. There wasn't much in the story, just something about students and a few faculty members picketing the ROTC building and blocking the doors. No names were given. I cut out the article and saved it, feeling foolish. Then I thought of the other women all over the country who must be building up similar files on their husbands and children. The same people who used to save clippings of their sons and daughters getting citizenship awards or starring in the school play.

I wonder whether N minded having his picture taken. When I take part in demonstrations, the photographers bother me more than anything else. I'm not really upset by the onlookers who shout or mutter things. Like the other people with me, I find myself straining to hear. "What did he say? What was that?" runs down the line of demonstrators, even when what is shouted can only be an insult, even when it's hurled from a car decorated with flapping American flags and patriotic bumper stickers. " 'Tell it to Hanoi,' I think he said," a man next to me will venture. "Or it may have been 'Go back to Hanoi.' "

But the picture-takers are unnerving even if they're friendly. Most of us, as individuals, don't want to be on television any more than we want to be in a government file.

I have to remind myself that I was the one who got N involved in politics in the first place. When I first knew him, he couldn't understand about people in New England. He was amazed at the way they're always calling up their legislators or running around with petitions. I think he thought at first that it was just me. I remember one time on election day when I asked him to stand with me in a group of people handing out campaign literature at the polls. The weather was raw, and I had just gotten over pneumonia. N not only refused to go himself but tried to prevent me.

"Just how much good do you think you're going to

do?" he asked me. "Do you think anybody is even going to notice you? What if you faint?"

"Then someone will notice me." A smart remark that I couldn't resist. He knows very well how much I hate feeling faint in public; my idea of hell is finding myself sitting in a circle of strangers, with that cool prickling on my forehead and dots of light wavering in front of my eyes, and hearing distant voices ordering me to put my head between my knees.

So I went out without my scarf because he was watching, and I didn't faint but did come home more tired than I would let him see. And I had intended to be an invalid for a few more days and let him do the dishes.

So different from that time last fall when I was sick again, in bed with a fever, and he couldn't understand why I let the farm workers down.

He rushed to the telephone, but it was for me. "The grape people want you to picket tomorrow."

"I can't. I just can't do it any more this year." He hadn't covered the mouthpiece.

"Well, picketing isn't for everyone, they say."

"You know I did it before." I sat up under the blankets.

"Then why can't you again?" His voice was louder until he remembered the receiver still lying in his hand. "Hello? She's awfully sorry, but she has other commitments. Try her again, though. Oh, any time, she'll be glad to." He hung up.

"How cruel," I said. "That boy spends his life on the telephone, and he's turned down by 90 percent of the people he calls. 95. Why should you add to his burden just to annoy me?"

"Because I suppose I haven't given up on you.

Maybe you'll say yes next time." He sounded so pious that I laughed. "Why can't you picket any more? Why did you ever do it, anyway? What were you doing, gathering material?"

That is the charge I can never answer, because it might be partly true.

N is tired of my being sick so much. He couldn't be more tired of it than I am.

When he first knew me, he used to worry when I got bronchitis. I didn't worry. It probably accounted for my interest in books, I told him. In our youth H and I spent much of every winter in bed, with the vaporizer bubbling and whichever one of us could breathe better reading aloud from *The Complete Sherlock Holmes*. We didn't enjoy being sick, but we made the best of it.

He was shocked. "It's terrible. Your parents should have done something."

"What could they do? My father felt guilty, of course, because he knew it was hereditary. He gets bronchitis too, but he tries to ignore it. You get used to it, and when you're well, you wonder what's missing."

After we were married and when N found that in spite of fever and alarming wheezing sounds I always recovered, I think he actually enjoyed my bronchitis; it made me romantic and mysterious, like Violetta. If he woke up in the morning on the narrow bed we shared that winter in Oxford and felt waves of heat coming from my side of the bed, he would touch my forehead and admire my bright eyes. Then he would sigh fondly and get up to fix me a glass of orange squash. It was at least two years before he got bored with all that. Now he can't stand my being sick and thinks of it as a trick I play to get out of obligations.

But this is misleading, and I see I have been misled as much as anyone. Because most of the time now I am well. A lot of bronchitis that year in England, true, but afterwards only a few colds every winter and the usual flu if it comes around. Until this last year, when one thing led to another and I seemed to be sick all the time. And it was true in the last year or so, I think, that the reasons weren't all physical. First there was all the work of writing the *Household* story and revising it for publication. "It wrote itself," I think I remember saying to someone at a party when I was impersonating an author. Not true; *I* wrote it, and it was a lot of work. Then came the McCarthy campaign, when all of us were too hopeful until the Chicago convention suddenly made us feel as if we had been knocked down and dragged through the streets by some monstrous engine. It was only a short while later that Mrs. Reginald Marsden found out about my book and told everyone. The fuss about it was entertaining for her, I guess, but not for me, and I started catching colds. Then the election. Unlike many of the people I know, I thought it still made a difference who won. (N didn't vote.) In January came the shock of realizing, along with a lot of other shocked people, that Richard Nixon was actually the President. I had no resistance to any kind of germ and got the flu, started to get well, and had a relapse. Then there was N and his involvement in politics, campus and otherwise. After that came my pneumonia, which drove him into a fury. The uncertainty about his term off and our trip to New Mexico didn't help.

* * *

I told Kurt part of this today when we went for the straw. What is his background? He never talks about it.

The pueblo was a surprise, though it shouldn't have been. I knew from pictures that it was the one in all the Social Studies books—stacked-up boxes with flat roofs on different levels, punctuated by windows, ladders, and round ends of roof beams. An antique Habitat. But I had thought of it as belonging only in a book, and real people live there. The church has a statue of the Virgin dressed in satin and sequins. A few pieces of lumpy, misshapen pottery for sale, made for the tourists because they expect pottery from Indians. The Pueblo Indians are farmers.

I'll have to sift the straw. It comes from the floor of a stable and is full of lumps of dried manure. We found a man to plaster my ceiling too. (Mr. Romero. Indians have Spanish names.) The spaces between the beams will be white plaster instead of dark brown boards with loose dirt filtering through the cracks. K referred to the plasterer as a drunken Indian, and I was shocked. But it's true, K said—he's a good plasterer when sober, doesn't come to work when drunk. And as proof, on our way home he pointed out Mr. Romero's car when we passed the bar on my corner. An assortment of weathered vehicles is always parked outside it at all hours of the afternoon and evening, and I can hear a jukebox and faint Spanish voices whenever I drive by.

June 23, 1969

Dear Nat—

I think I saw a picture of you the other day, but I might be wrong. Maybe you weren't in that crowd, shouting something. Maybe instead you were at your desk, busy transforming Dickens's Techniques in Characterization *into* Dickens as a Social Reformer. *Have you ever thought how fortunate it was that you decided, finally, against doing your dissertation on the novels of Swinburne? I'm very nasty, I see, but it was a shock to me last fall to find you suddenly admiring all the sentimental passages that both of us had deplored in the past. Your new chapter touchingly titled "The Death of Smike," for instance; had you really forgotten about our neighbor's dog in Bloomington, the one we secretly named Smike because he was so dim-witted and obsequious?*

It's funny that it should be comforting not to know whether you are getting my letters. It makes me reckless in what I write because I know that after I have mailed one and begun to regret what I've said, I can think, well, he probably won't get it after all. And when you don't answer, as you don't, I can assume that you are writing to me all the time. My mailbox thief tears up your letters and throws them away. Kurt is right, of course, in advising me to rent a box in the Post Office. Maybe I will.

But you don't know who Kurt is, do you?

A.

June 23, 1969

Dear Nat—

I will mail this at the Post Office and assume you will receive it.

Is this the first letter you've had from me? Not knowing the answer to that question, I don't know where to begin. I can't explain all over again about the house until I've heard from you. Write to me, please, at least once.

I send all the love I have left.

Anne

June 24

Fireplace day. The whole procedure was so simple that I am stunned. I bought some adobe bricks, also fireproof tiles for the chimney, then picked up Maria Archuleta and her teen-age daughter Carmen, my fireplace builders. They brought a wooden trough, a trowel, a short-handled hoe, and a hatchet. Maria was large and silent, Carmen languid and useless-looking. After chopping an alarming hole in the roof, Maria put the fireplace and chimney together, brick by brick. She worked so confidently that I had to assume she knew what she was doing. Carmen mixed mud in the trough and helped her mother slap it on and lift the bricks into place, chewing gum the whole time and singing Beatles tunes in a Spanish accent ("Ah-ee wun do hole you hahnd") .

And now there is a rough curved fireplace in the corner by the window, just like the sketch I drew for Maria—raised about eighteen inches above the floor, with ledges of brick leading up the sides where the fireplace meets the wall. I'll plaster it later, when I do the walls. I have always understood that there's a lot more than this to building a proper fireplace. "Are you sure it will draw?" I asked Maria.

She stared at me and shrugged. "Thirty-five dollars," she said.

I paid her and drove both Archuletas home. I haven't the slightest doubt that the fireplace will draw.

June 25

My flagstones have come, delivered two days ago by Mr. Velasquez in a dilapidated truck which drove down all the wrong roads before he finally found the way to my house. K and I could see him going past each time, and we and Angie Ortega and all the little boys in the neighborhood signaled frantically at him to get him to go back to the river and start over. Each time he waved to us, went on till he found a turning-around place, and bumped down the road again, nodding a greeting as he went past. It took him four tries to find my road. He was a great success with my neighbors who, except Angie, shake their heads over my house-repair project. He doesn't approve of my putting the stones inside the house; they're meant for a patio, he explained. But there's nothing he can do about it if I choose to do something so crazy with them, he told the little boys, making "crazy" gestures toward me.

The stones are dark red and all shapes, and they lean in rows against the front of the house like my stack of extra adobe bricks. Why not have stone book shelves, laid across piled bricks and running along the wall next to the fireplace, then turning at a right angle to partition the room at the head of the bed? There are enough long, thin stones. I can start tomorrow.

Mozart–Concerto 23–Gieseking. Notes dropping into place inevitably, gently. What if I had to choose between N and Mozart? One of them being born, I mean. He's right; I don't love him as much as he needs to be loved.

Because it isn't only politics that comes between us.

N has always been too easy for me to hurt. So often I have to be careful of the expression on my face in case he should misunderstand it. He is especially sensitive if I am writing. If he comes into the room suddenly and asks me a question and I look up in irritation or even abstraction, he can't stand it. I seem to him to be proving something he has always known.

And then the mornings when he doesn't have to be at the college, when, wearing only his pajama pants, he comes up behind me as I sit at the desk and puts his hands on my shoulders and lets them slide down to my breasts and waits for me to respond in some way. (He never says anything then, just stands there, so I don't know how to answer him.) There are some mornings, of course, when I would welcome any distraction, but he doesn't seem to be so much attracted to me then. I don't suppose N has ever consciously tried to prevent me from working, but sometimes when he sees how much energy I direct toward my writing, he is drawn to me and can't keep away. At those times the morning is ruined whatever I do. I can make him go away with only a look or a stiffening of my shoulders or an absence of response, but his anger or mortification will reverberate through the apartment and through my head for the rest of that day and keep me from accomplishing anything. If I give up and go to bed with him, my resentment leads to cold defeat for both of us.

I claim to think of my writing as not much more than a joke, and yet sometimes I put it before everything else. How contradictory. It's true that I would not even have thought of writing the first book if N hadn't talked me into it, but since that time, perhaps, I have begun to change.

N compared me once last winter to a woman we know who does ceramics and neglects her family. She has put herself on a strict schedule and spends her days throwing pots while her sons wreck the neighborhood. I don't wholly admire her, though they are lovely pots. She should manage better.

3

June 26

I saw a new side of Seth today. H was standing in the open door of his studio when I drove up. She waved to me, and I went to join her and looked through the doorway. The three children, as well as some of their friends from the neighborhood, were sitting in a loose circle on the floor of the studio, busily gluing little blocks of wood onto boards in patterns. S was going from one child to another, giving advice and praise. Everyone looked happy, even Seth.

"How did you get him to do it?" I asked.

H was surprised. "Oh, it's his class. He does it every week, just for fun. He's a wonderful teacher."

Seth clapped his hands. "All right, everybody." He held up a large container of Elmer's Glue, and the children ran up to him one by one, dipped their fingers into it, and then walked around the room waving their hands carefully in the air. They looked ecstatic.

"It's their favorite game," H said. "They let it dry and peel it off afterwards. They're only allowed to do it at the end of the class or they'd use up all the glue."

There are no absolutes, I keep reminding myself.

* * *

I wish Bronson weren't such a good friend of Seth. He comes and sits in the kitchen waiting for Seth and talking to H, and the way he looks at me makes me uncomfortable. As if he understands exactly what I am and doesn't approve. Knowing that he doesn't understand me is no help at all. I still feel that I have to justify myself for being different from H, even for looking different from her.

Kurt, by contrast, is restful. His idea of me is no more accurate than Bronson's, but he makes me better than I am instead of worse.

June 27

H and I had a terrible quarrel this morning, such a bad one that I don't see how I can face her again. She had come to help build my bookshelves, and we were in the living room, surrounded by adobe bricks, flagstones, and containers of mud. We built up the first layers of bricks easily and found that my bookcase idea would work. Building with adobe is like playing with blocks. I can see why so many people here can't let their houses alone.

We started out by discussing Kurt. "He was married to a countess," H said, "among others."

After my initial surprise, I could picture her. Elegant, with complicated hair and an accent. "You said *was*. Isn't he married anymore?" I wondered how Kurt could admire other women after being married to a countess.

"I don't know. He may be." She looked at me. "Why? Does it matter?"

"No, I was just wondering. He never talks about her."

"He has some children somewhere, too. There's a rumor that he lives on alimony, but I don't think it's true. He gets a disability check from the Government every month because he went crazy in the Army, and he does sell paintings. It's hard to imagine Kurt married, actually."

"He's so self-sufficient," I said.

"Yes, and he's too much everybody's friend to stick to a family of his own. He likes Spanish people, Indians, women, everybody exotic. Even the hippies. Most of the artists can't stand them at all, but Kurt actually thinks they're interesting. He sincerely loves people. On the other hand, he never gets seriously involved with anybody. He always manages to detach himself, and then he can go home and look out at the Gorge and meditate or see visions or paint or whatever he wants to do."

"So he's never lonely."

"I don't think he is." H was sitting back on her heels in front of the bookcase with her hands upturned in her lap. The leaves on the poplar trees outside the big window shone in the sun, and the irrigation ditch made little rippling noises. "I wish I could be that way," she said. "Sometimes I like being alone, but mostly I don't even feel alive unless someone else is there. There are times when I'm afraid to look in the mirror because I'm sure there won't be a reflection." Her voice was high and tense.

I wondered what I could say to make her feel better. "Maybe that's why you were such a good actress. Because you needed to make contact with people, and the audience could feel it." I realized too late that I had used the past tense.

"Yes, I was, wasn't I?" She turned away and began to pack mud into a chink between two bricks.

I saw Tomas standing in the doorway. He had begged to come along and help build the shelves but had lost interest quickly and gone outside to play. He looked restless and was carrying his BB gun.

"Tomas, why don't you leave your gun outside?" I asked him in my mildest voice. I had heard H tell him that he mustn't bring it into the house.

He didn't appear to hear me. He lifted the gun and began to aim at various objects—the Japanese paper lampshade, the tall candle on the fireplace shelf, the green bottle on the window sill. He glanced at H, who didn't see him. Then he smiled faintly at me and moved the gun until it was pointing at my face. He sighted along it, checking his aim.

He was still paying no attention. "Tomas, please put that away," I said, trying to sound casual.

H jerked around to look at Tomas. He held the gun innocently at his side now, pointing at the floor. He was still smiling at me. "What's the matter?" H said. "He wasn't doing any harm, was he?" She was glaring at me, and her voice was unsteady.

"It's just one of my rules," I said. "No guns in the house." I had broken one of my rules myself: Never correct someone else's children if the parents are within hearing.

"Tomasito." H went to him and put her arm across his shoulders, leaving mud tracks. "You'd better go outside. It's obvious you aren't wanted in here."

"He can stay," I said, although I knew it wouldn't do any good.

"Go on, dear." H shoved Tomas toward the door, and he gave her a pathetic look and ran out. "Poor little thing," she said.

"Couldn't you see what he was doing?" I asked. H has complained often enough about Tomas's habit of trying to get her attention by deliberate bad behavior. "Didn't you see him pointing his gun at me? And I didn't speak sharply to him."

"He's only a child! Don't you know anything about children? Just because you were smart enough not to have any of your own! Did you have to hurt him like that?"

"I wasn't the one who told him he wasn't wanted."

"You think I've made a mess of my life, don't you?" Tears were streaming down H's face, and she couldn't control her mouth. She sat down on the window ledge, shattered and sobbing. "At least the things I do are real and they're human. I don't plan everything."

I know that my sister doesn't cry on purpose. H has gone through life breaking down in front of teachers, boyfriends, and traffic policemen, and it's something she hates doing. It makes her ugly, and it alarms people who don't know her well, but she can't help it. I told myself this, but it didn't do much good. When H cries, I have never been able to do anything but pray for her to stop. "I know what you think about my children," she said. "You think they're wild and aggressive and I don't discipline them enough. They make you nervous, don't they? Whenever they touch anything of yours, you're afraid they'll break it. Don't you think it's obvious how you feel?"

I shook my head. But part of what she said was true.

"You think Tomas shouldn't be allowed to have a gun, don't you? Well, I hate it as much as you do, but do you realize that if I didn't let him have it, he would be the only boy in our neighborhood without one?" She tried to laugh. "And it's only a BB gun. Most of them have .22s. I don't want my children to have to be different. They have to grow up someday, and I want them to be strong. Do you think I want them to turn out like us?" Wisps of hair stuck to H's wet cheeks, and her face was streaked with mud. "What right do you have to criticize other people's lives? Is yours so perfect? Your own husband is trying so hard to be popular with his students that he can't be bothered to pay any attention to you."

The attack on N took me by surprise. "That isn't why he supports them." I was as angry now as H could possibly be. "Nat would never do anything in bad faith. He cares about teaching and about his students. He cares so much. You don't know him."

H went to the door and called Tomas. "We're going home now. Come on, honey. Good-bye," she said to me.

I don't know whether or not to go to the LeFevres' party tonight. H and Seth will be there, and I don't think I can stand a continuation of the quarrel; as it is, I know I'll spend the rest of the afternoon arguing with her in my mind.

June 28

Luminarios. Ordinary brown grocery bags with the edges folded over to make a rim. Each bag half-filled with sand, and a lighted candle stuck into it. The whole thing gives off a soft orange glow. The Le-Fevres' house is built around a patio with a *portal* on three sides, and they had placed *luminarios* all along the edge of the roof. The only other light came from a bonfire in the middle of the patio.

Funny people. Herman LeFevre is one of the more successful artists in town—sells sculpture and is often an artist-in-residence, etc. Cornelia devoted her life to protecting him and furthering his career. Both of them are small, agile, and brown like monkeys, with white hair and friendly crinkled eyes. It might be hard to tell them apart if Cornelia didn't wear her hair in a long white braid. H is contemptuous, but they mean well, I think.

Cornelia was wearing a squash-blossom necklace and seven turquoise bracelets. She gripped my hand as soon as I arrived and led me to a bench set against the outside wall of the house. "Why don't you sit down here, next to . . . uh . . . Gretchen?" Then she dashed to the gate to greet someone else. I saw Gretchen McKinney looking up at me with a wry expression.

"So Cornelia knows my name," Gretchen said. "I would not have thought I was useful enough for her to remember me."

I was looking around for H and Seth but couldn't see them. I sat down by Gretchen. "Bronson is very angry," she said, pointing.

"Why?" I saw Bronson pacing moodily around the fire.

"Because the LeFevres invited us to this party. They expect a New York art critic, and we are all here to provide atmosphere. Picturesque, is it not?"

I couldn't deny it. Everyone was wearing a costume, and the background looked like a stage set. Someone in a corner of the *portal* was playing an accordion. I was glad I had worn the black Mexican skirt and the new green stole that reminds me of the mountains. "Why did Bronson come, then?" I asked her.

"Why did any of them come? They want to sell their paintings or their poems or whatever they make. And it is a party. These are people who work alone. They need to see other people sometimes."

"Yes, of course."

"Is Kurt not here?" Gretchen was looking at me curiously.

"I don't know. I don't see him." It was so dark that it was hard to recognize most of the guests. I wondered whether people were beginning to pair me off with Kurt in their minds.

"He is so kind, you know. He has been teaching me to drive." Gretchen laughed and held up her hand, the fingers spread out. "For five years. I have no gift for it. He says I am a born pedestrian. When I come to a crossroad, I always stop the car and look both ways, and there is Kurt beside me shouting 'Go on! You have the right of way!' Bronson says I am too stupid to learn, but Kurt keeps trying. At least it is a chance for me to get out of the house."

"I think you'll learn." I hadn't realized she was so much a prisoner.

"In Vienna, where I lived before, there was no need to drive." Gretchen sighed, and her medieval face looked sad.

I wondered why I had been intimidated by Gretchen the night I met her, and why she had always seemed to me so serene and sure of herself. Maybe only because Kurt described her that way just before introducing her. Gretchen isn't serene. She looked skinny and dejected in her flowered dirndl last night, like the Constant Nymph or somebody's *au pair* girl.

Gretchen and I watched Cornelia arranging her guests. Her husband sat near the door to the house, smiling behind his pipe and looking like her twin brother, brown and clever under his white hair. "Aren't they lucky to have found each other," I said.

"Yes, indeed. She is the secret of his success."

"I couldn't imagine either of them married to anyone else."

"Ah, but they were. This is the second marriage for her, the third for him. They have been together perhaps ten years, not more."

"But they look just alike!" Is nothing to be depended upon?

Gretchen shrugged. "They will stay together, I think. Cornelia is a manager. The other two wives were artists, and there was conflict. Artists should not marry other artists."

"I suppose that's true, but they do it all the time. I wonder why."

Gretchen looked at me with her round brown eyes. "Ignorance, perhaps. No one can know beforehand what a marriage will be like. If a young girl has a talent, she is naturally attracted to a man who can understand that talent. But I think there is sometimes cowardice too. Perhaps she is not really sure that she will do well as a painter or musician or whatever, and she marries a man who will take the risks instead. If her husband succeeds in his art, she can share that success. If he fails, it is sad and she may feel that she has wasted her own gift. But she can never know that she surely would have failed, because she has not tried."

"But can't both of them succeed?"

"Very seldom, I think." Gretchen looked across the

courtyard, where I now saw H and Seth standing together.

I wondered whether Gretchen had been talking about H as well as herself. H, looking fragile in an embroidered blouse, her loose dark hair streaming down, was clinging to Seth's arm and gazing up at his face while he talked to a man in striped pants and a new pink cowboy shirt. The New York critic, undoubtedly. I had no reason, I told myself, to assume that H was being hypocritical. She really was proud of Seth as a painter. Her complaints to me were only about his personal behavior. She saw me and waved happily. "Hi. Are you in a better mood?" she called.

I should have known that H would have recovered from our quarrel by then. Each time I have fought with her in the past, it has seemed to me that things were being said that would make it impossible for us ever again to feel any affection for each other, and I have felt broken and lamed afterwards, sometimes for weeks or more. But then, always, when I see H again, she appears not to know that anything wrong has happened between us. Each quarrel seems at the time to be different from all the others, so I can never benefit from past experience. It isn't that H doesn't bear grudges; her accusations during our arguments prove that there is a permanent and growing catalogue of my offenses in some part of her mind. But her hate is no more to be depended on than her love. Did she love Seth last night? She was looking at him as if she did, and I could see the art critic envying Seth his ideal marriage. Just by looking at H then, anyone could tell that she picked fresh flowers every day and baked her own bread.

It was after eleven o'clock. Cornelia circulated, managing her party. Then Kurt appeared out of the dark beyond the gate, escorting a tall, solid woman. "Greetings," he said. "This is Katrin."

"Peace," Katrin said in a deep voice. Seen only in outline, she looked middle-aged, but as she came into the light I saw that she couldn't be more than twenty. Part of her bulk was accounted for by the knapsack on her back, the guitar slung from one shoulder, and the baby in her arms, but she was still very large. She wore a poncho over a long red skirt, and her large feet were bare.

"Katrin was hitchhiking," Kurt said. "Isn't she wonderful?"

"Kurt, we are all wonderful." Katrin's voice was low, slow, and musical. She sat down, tucked the edge of her poncho under the baby, and unbuttoned her blouse. Then she took out an enormous breast and began to feed the baby. Katrin was on her way to a commune in the hills, Kurt explained, but he had persuaded her to come to the party with him. Her head was small for her body, I noticed, and her blond hair was cropped unevenly. Her features were pure and delicate, like those of an angel on a Christmas card. When she had finished feeding the baby, she took out her guitar and sang folk songs in a baritone voice while Cornelia beamed.

Gretchen, with her talk of driving lessons, was trying to warn me against misinterpreting Kurt. He is kind to everyone, I think she was telling me; don't take it personally. But that's why I like him, because there's no chance of his becoming too much involved with me and of my having to reject him. I suppose H was warning me too, by talking about his wives yesterday afternoon before Tomas came in.

Emma, on having no children of her own: "I shall be very well off, with all the children of a sister I love so much to care about. There will be enough of them, in all probability, to supply every sort of sensation that declining life can need."

Every sort of sensation. I do love H's children when they are only themselves, when she isn't there to force me to see them through the screen of her emotions. In H's presence I can't speak directly to Melisande, for instance, without H suspecting me of hidden criticism. When I was trying to help the children with their mobile, H looked at me every time I made a suggestion, and finally she said, "Why don't you let them do it themselves?" So of course I stopped interfering. Maybe that's what I was doing, but I don't think so. After that, Nora kept on asking me for advice, and I didn't know what to say.

H knows herself better than I thought she did. Her remark earlier, about the mirror, stunned me because it made me remember how important mirrors used to be to her when we were growing up. She would sit in front of her dressing table, sometimes holding a hand mirror up so she could see herself from unaccustomed angles. "I'm so beautiful," she would say to me. "Can you see how beautiful I am? I mustn't waste it."

H is exhausted by her children partly because she sees them as extensions of herself. When the children were small, she says, for a long time she could tell exactly what they were thinking. Because she knew the whole context of their lives, every syllable of baby talk meant something to her, and she could often anticipate what they would do or say. This isn't true any longer, but she says herself that at times it is hard for her to realize it. How distracting it must be to be responsible for the existence of three human beings. I can try to imagine how it must feel, but I don't think I can even come close.

Maybe H thinks of me as if I hadn't grown up. She seems to expect me always to be in some kind of childish race with her, as if I had no life separate from hers. But she has made (is making) her own life, and I am making mine. Marianne and Elinor again, sensibility and sense; H can't bear what she regards as my coolness, my efficiency.

I left out something in what I wrote about H's visit home just before I got married, probably because I still haven't gotten over the embarrassment I felt at the time. It was on the day before the wedding, I think, that my two little nieces went into my room and unpacked my going-away suitcase, complete with matching white lace nightgown and negligee and my first perfume and the little zipped case with the diaphragm equipment and the coy instructions that I caught Melisande attempting to read to Nora. H had seen them go in but hadn't stopped them, then was blazingly indignant when I put them out of the room. ("What do you expect of children?" as they clung to her skirt and she held the baby in front of her like a shield.) For the rest of the day she kept trying to get me to kiss them, and by the next morning she seemed to have forgotten.

I remember her wedding so much more clearly than my own. The actual ceremony (mine) isn't there in my mind at all. I do recall that I was disguised as a bride in N's mother's veil of fragile antique lace (sure that I would step on it, and sure enough, I did—two holes for my mother to invisibly mend before she sent it back). My bouquet was made of stiff white Fuji chrysanthemums, I remember, and when I was still holding it after the ceremony, standing at the head of the stairs in the parish hall and wondering who I was supposed to throw it to, I shook it slightly and the petals started to fall off. I kept shaking it then for some reason, and the petals rattled down like rice onto the stairway while my mother stood looking pained and gesturing to me to stop because I was littering the church. The bouquet that Joanne finally caught wasn't much but a bundle of bare green stems.

June 29

If my parents hadn't moved away from the house where I grew up. If N were with me now or if I knew at least that he wanted to be. Or if he and I had ever lived in one place for longer than three years. If we owned a house together. If H and Seth were happy.

If just one of those things were true, I might lose this feeling of floating.

I tried taking up part of the linoleum today, but had to replace it when I found there was too much loose dirt to sweep away or pack down. Will have to wait till I can lay my flagstones. I've started to work on the living-room ceiling, scrubbing the *vigas* with detergent and sand and nailing chicken wire to the boards between them. I was right to buy the house, I think, but there are far too many changes I have to make in it and too many mistakes I won't be able to avoid.

* * *

The day my parents moved out of the parsonage, just about a year ago. N and I went to help them transport breakable things to the house they had rented in a town on the shore about forty miles north of Boston. It was a sadder day than it needed to be because not only were my parents leaving the house, but the church was abandoning it too. The new minister, on his first visit to town, had inspected the parsonage and found it the wrong setting for himself and his mod wife. There was no point in being sentimental about a Victorian barn with bad plumbing, he said, and he went to a real-estate agent and found a trim new imitation-Colonial house that the church could buy for $5,000 more than they could get for the old one. The trustees, limp with surprise, approved the switch, and the old parsonage was sold several months before the new minister moved to town.

My family had loved the house so much that somehow I guess we must have been under the impression that it was ours. There was a big front porch and two small, unexpected balconies outside upstairs windows. A turret on one corner of the house made a round alcove in the living room and upstairs study and a round closet in H's room above. One of the two fireplaces was faced with glazed brown tiles and had a grinning bronze ogre's face set just above the opening (the King of the Golden River). On the day of the move I sat on the window seat on the landing and looked out onto the greening lawn and listened to my mother. She was giving a rather hypocritical description of the new minister's wife in her little leather skirt and false eyelashes. ("Poor little thing. The Alliance ladies are going to eat her alive. Still, I suppose there isn't any reason in the world why she shouldn't dress like a high-school girl.") I noticed then that the bullet hole was still there. Well, of course it was. The tiny round hole wouldn't have let in enough air to persuade the trustees to replace a piece of plate glass that big. Not if they wouldn't even get the shower fixed.

The house showed up well, even that day, when there was nothing in it but the boxes and furniture separated into groups for Morgan Memorial, the Salvation Army, and the church library. The ceilings were high, and the stairs were wide. The house was bare, shabby, and filled with sunlight. We were lucky to spend so many years there, and there is no point in wishing we still had that house to go back to, with the same neighborhood and friends we had known for at least part of our lives. I suppose that kind of stability is overrated by those of us who don't have it. Angie Ortega has never been further away from here than Santa Fe, and she and Luis are distant cousins, related to half the people in town. Yet she feels suffocated by her family, she says, and she is always eager to meet strangers.

Angie's life is really no more secure than H's or mine. Luis never keeps a job for long because he has a bad temper. (That's hard to believe from what I see of him, waving to me on his way to or from his truck. He is courtly and gentle behind his savage Aztec face, and he brings me lettuce from his garden. He has decided I am harmless, Angie reports, in spite of his forebodings when he first saw my desert boots and old jeans.) He finds jobs easily because electricians are scarce, but his employers always, sooner or later, offend his pride, and he gathers his tools and stalks out, threatening to move to Salt Lake City. He throws wrenches at people when he is angry but always misses, she says, and sometimes he comes home from the bar on the corner with a black eye. He has never hurt Angie, but she assumes he would if she gave him reason. "He is a good man," she says, "but he has his pride."

June 30, 1969

Dear Nat—

Your mother's birthday is next week. The 6th. Have you forgotten? You always did.

Do you add up the check stubs yourself now? Make your own dental appointments? Change the toilet-paper rolls? You never noticed that anyone did those things. They just happened.

Are you well?

A.

June 30

There is no reason why I shouldn't be allowed to use my mailbox. It's there, and I have a right to put letters into it without expecting them to be stolen. Besides, I think the thief may have given up. In the last week I have received, intact, three ads and a letter from my parents.

Still, there may have been other mail. I have a clear mental picture of a man opening the box, taking out a letter from N, searching it for money, and stuffing it into his pocket to throw away later. He can't read the letter because it isn't in Spanish. A few days ago, around mail delivery time, I saw my thief shambling along in the distance as I was turning onto the main road after crossing the bridge. I was almost sure, but I didn't turn around and try to find out whether I was right.

* * *

My garlic plants are almost waist high now, with curving white blossoms like the tilted, beaked heads of birds. I walked through them to the mailbox this morning, and I had just finished raising the flag and was talking to the little boys who fish from the bridge when I saw Kurt's station wagon bumping down the road, flashing sunlight from all its chrome trimmings. Kurt jumped out and opened the door for Katrin, who climbed slowly out with her baby bundled in her arms. She wanted to see my house, Kurt said. I saw that she was gazing toward it, with a small, firm smile.

I have fallen into the habit of visualizing this house as it will be when I've finished working on it. I see it with a covered *portal* and a flagstone terrace leading around one side. Perhaps the front, under the roof of the *portal,* will be painted white as I have seen it on several other houses. The window frames and the door will be a deep blue, and there will be a brass lion-head knocker on the door. The hollyhocks will be thick and high, in several colors.

This morning, looking at the house through Katrin's eyes, I saw that it's still only a large, square hut with staring windows and a crooked doorway opening directly out into a yard crowded with stacked flagstones and adobe bricks, piles of sand and gravel, and a roll of chicken wire. The only improvements that show from the outside are the lopsided screen door and the temporary doorstep I've made by dragging three cement blocks from Kurt's trash pile to the area in front of the door and covering them with one of the flagstones. The few hollyhocks I have now are white and spindly. The one red one was trampled by the man who delivered the bricks, and I haven't been able to revive it. I started to explain all this but stopped suddenly, afraid I was babbling, when Katrin didn't respond.

"Isn't it beautiful, Katrin?" Kurt said.

Katrin shifted the baby to her other shoulder and smiled.

Inside, although I haven't accomplished much more, my plans for the future of the house are more apparent. The shapes of things are almost as they will be. When Kurt lived here, the stove was on one side of the kitchen and the crude, high table on the other, both as far as possible from the sink. The table is a counter now, just inside the door at right angles to the sink, with the stove against the wall near it. My new cedar picnic table and benches are on the other side of the doorway, under Kurt's moonlight painting. "There will be a flagstone floor," I explained to Katrin, "and I'm going to plaster the walls with light-colored mud, and the ceiling will be white between the *vigas*." I led the way into the second room and showed them the ceiling. The beams are blond in the corner where I've worked, and strips of chicken wire are stretched over the dark boards between them, waiting for the plaster.

"Ah," Katrin gave a deep, female sigh as she stood in the doorway and saw the big window. "Kurt, there is your window." She was as solid as a mother in a Picasso painting, I thought.

"It's a wonderful window," I said. Kurt has put two windows like it into his new house, he tells me.

Katrin walked into the living room and rotated slowly, looking around. The ceiling light bulbs at least have shades now, and the fireplace and bookshelves are in place, though unplastered. The walls still look wounded, with their nail-holes and scratches in the places where the racks were. "I'm going to get an Indian print bedspread," I said, "and some extra ones to make curtains." I was afraid that if I didn't tell her these things, she wouldn't see what a beautiful house it is.

Katrin wandered over to the fireplace and reached out to stroke the rough, unchinked bricks. "Ah," she said again. Then she turned to me. "Why do you want to change everything?" she asked. "This is so beautiful. Why not leave it as it is?"

"The fireplace?" I was really puzzled.

"The fireplace, everything." Katrin indicated the room with a circular motion of her small, round head. "Why not accept it as it is and simply allow it to be beautiful?" Kurt nodded, gazing at her. "Why put up curtains?" Katrin said. "Why not let Nature come into the room—the sunlight, the clouds, the darkness. Are you afraid of Nature?"

I was too dishonest to answer that. "Not necessarily, I said. "Just of little boys walking past the window while I'm taking a bath."

"And you mind that." Katrin looked wonderingly at me.

"Yes, I do." I kept myself from adding, "It's the way I was brought up."

She chuckled. To my relief, the baby began to cry then, in thin, mewing gasps, and Katrin sat down on the mattress under the window and began to unwrap him. "Amos, little Amos," she said in a low, humming tone.

"Amos?" I looked toward Kurt to see whether I had heard right.

He nodded. I thought immediately that I would never have named a baby that, and then was annoyed at myself. What right have I, with a nice, plain name myself, to criticize what other people call their children?

The baby, unrolled from his layers of blankets, was small and thin, with a bluish, shrewd-looking face. He stared up at me with sharp eyes as I came closer. I could see a vein throbbing in his bare scalp. "How old is he?" I asked. I couldn't venture a compliment on his looks, although I know that the usual standards of infant beauty don't apply to brand-new babies.

"Six months," Katrin said, and I was startled again. I wouldn't have guessed that the baby was more than two weeks old. But then, I wouldn't know.

Katrin pulled a yellow-stained diaper out from under the baby's tiny hips as he waved shiny dark legs, mottled like sausages. "Good boy, Amos," she said, and flung the diaper to the floor. She chuckled and lit a cigarette, narrowing her eyes against the smoke. The cigarette should have looked incongruous, I thought, but it didn't; it simply made Katrin seem more worldly and possibly more human. Looking at Katrin's heavy ankles and feet placed so firmly on the floor under the folds of her red skirt, I felt strangely insubstantial—too slight and unfeminine in my shirt and old tan slacks.

Now I know how Gretchen felt when I gushed over her house. When Katrin said that about the bricks, I wished I were brave enough to mention the black widows that would make nests in the chinks. I dreaded her vast, amused smile. She would never be afraid of a spider and might even claim (I know she would) to think it was beautiful. A black widow can't even spin a decent web, I've noticed. The most messy, irregular spider webs I've ever seen. (There I go, criticizing again, even spiders.)

July 1

D.H. Lawrence writing to Mabel Dodge about Taos: "Is there a colony of rather dreadful sub-arty people?" Her book doesn't say how she answered that question.

I think it would be even harder to bring up children here than it is anywhere else now, because of the temptation to isolate them from everything ugly. The McKinneys make all their Christmas-tree ornaments out of yarn and sticks, H says, in spite of having a huge box of Gretchen's Austrian glass decorations put away somewhere. And Bronson threw out some folding aluminum chairs and made his family sit on the floor for two years until he could build some handsome wooden ones. Bronson is a product of this kind of upbringing. Until he was about eight his mother scandalized her Spanish neighbors by letting him run naked in summer. In winter he wore little wool smocks and breeches that she wove for him. She taught him at home till he was old enough to be sent off to an Eastern progressive school where he learned things like sheepshearing and madrigal singing. By the time he grew up, he was so suspicious of the outside world that he was unfitted to live anywhere but here. Bronson's mother, luckily for him, left him plenty of money to support his tastes. Now he is treating his own children the same way, and so are many of the other Anglos in town, including H and S.

I can't really blame them, especially for trying to shield their children from television. "Do you think I want them to turn into advertising machines," H says, "reciting commercials and begging for plastic toys?" I know what she means, but the effect is that television appeals to Nora and Tomas as a forbidden treat, and they sneak over to the neighbors' houses to watch as many programs as they can. (Melisande has passed out of that stage, and is a puritanical echo of H.) The other day H and the children came to my house to help me make scratches on the walls so the mud plaster will stick. Just the job for Tomas, I thought, but he lost interest quickly, and he and Nora went over to visit Angie, who keeps her television set going all day long for company. Nora came running back soon, excited and happy, to urge H to go to Angie's house too. "But it's a good program, Mummy," she said. "Come and watch. They're giving things away!"

H only smiled sadly at me, but Melisande said, in a withering tone, "Really, Nora, don't you know that watching television causes brain damage?" Failing to lure any of us, Nora ran back to her program, while Melisande kept on scratching the walls in a self-righteous way. If I were H, I don't know what I would do.

H says she hopes her children will be tough; she doesn't want them to be like us. But the trouble is that she doesn't really want them to be like other children either. She would be pleased if Melisande and Nora were popular with the children in their neighborhood, and yet the values she has taught them make that impossible. H's children can't help feeling superior to the Spanish children they see breaking their own family's rules of taste and economy. I don't know what H could have done about that. It might have helped if she had taught them Spanish instead of French, but how can I be sure even of that? She gave them French as something that was all their own.

H still surprises me sometimes by talking as if she expected to return to the Playhouse in a year or so and take over her old roles again, but something happened yesterday to show how unlikely she must know it is.

I had decided to go to Santa Fe to see the town and look at tiles, curtain material, etc. for the house. H and the children went with me, and I finally saw the Folk Art Museum and the Governor's Palace. We all had a good time, partly because of H's talent for making even the most ordinary shopping trip into an expedition. Then we went to the Chinese restaurant for dinner. (Tomas: "I hate Chinese food. Do I have to eat it?" and after dinner, "I'm hungry. What is there to eat?" But H and I both refused to rise to this, and no one was offended.) We had a good meal with too much to eat, and I showed them how to use chopsticks—one of the few useful things N learned in the Army. But after dinner there were fortune cookies, and of course we read the messages out loud. Mine was something about friendship, Nora's was about romance, Melisande's was about money, and Tomas must have eaten his because we couldn't find it. H's fortune seemed funny at first, as she read it out in a solemn voice: "You are vital to your career." She and I laughed at the way it was worded, and the children laughed because we were laughing. But then Nora, proud of sharing a grown-up joke and wanting to prolong it, said, in a joyful, penetrating voice, "But, Mummy, you don't have a career," and laughed harder than ever.

H always did change into someone else when she

cried—a swollen, blotchy-faced stranger—but now she looks worse; her face falls apart. The atmosphere in the car on the way back was so full of tension that even the children hardly dared to say anything.

We take it for granted, H and I, that she could just get on a stage and act, any time she wanted; everything would come back. But when I think of the panic I felt when I had finally finished the *Household* novel and let it go, the certainty I had that I could never do such a thing again, I wonder. She may feel that way about acting. She must. How long has it been?

An absurd dream last night, Katrin ostentatiously opening my screen door for a fly. "Flies are a part of Nature's plan," she explains. In reality, I am the one who lets flies out when they cluster on the screen. It's easier than swatting them.

Katrin sings in five languages—Spanish, Russian, French, German, Hebrew—besides English. The implication is that she speaks all these languages too.

"That baby is not right, do you think?" Angie said to me yesterday when Katrin had left. I didn't know Angie had even seen the baby, but she has those two big front windows and not much to watch besides the mountains. She couldn't have had more than a glimpse of poor little Amos. He looks unborn, that's it. Skinned, the way a little kangaroo must look. Not ready to be exposed to the air.

Why should I resent Katrin? I scarcely know her at all. But she has a way of showing up other people's flaws just by being the way she is. Am I the only one who feels this? Yes, evidently. Everyone else admires her, especially K.

* * *

Buy a toaster. One of those horizontal ones that can be used as an oven.

July 2

K made some comment about my hair today, saying he likes it now that it is longer. I, no more graceful about compliments than usual, explained that I am growing it out only because it won't curl in the dry air here. "Nat won't approve," I said unnecessarily. "He likes it short."

K looked at me. "Do you know that every time I say anything personal to you, you mention your husband?"

True. I hadn't noticed it myself.

What is N doing now? I went to the library to look through current newspapers, also bought papers in Santa Fe. Nothing. No mention of him or the college. So no trouble? Perhaps I should have registered the letter I mailed at the Post Office. (My game with the mailbox is beginning to pall.)

I could write to his parents, I suppose. Casually, of course, and talking about how hard he's working on his book. I would not, couldn't let them guess how little I know about what he's doing now. Surely he wouldn't have told them what has happened—not happened—between us? No, he doesn't tell them things.

N says that when he was a child his father bought a copy of *Who's Who* so that any time he might doubt his own eminence he could look himself up. But it isn't true. His mother bought it, and N used to look his father up. I have seen his father's eyes like cool gray water looking past me above his pipe; I have watched him assembling all his gray-green gear before one of his trips (waist-high waders, landing nets, tackle box, long aluminum fishing-pole cases, thermometers, compass, tent, ground cloth, and hundreds of other things, including a tough, dark molasses cake in a blackened tin), and I know that it could never have mattered to him at all what anyone might think of him or write about him and print in a book.

But N used to look him up, and that is what is important to N—his hard-luck story, his personal blacking factory. He grew up thinking he was the son of a famous man, just because his mother told him so. N has never even read any of his father's *Journals of a Naturalist;* he has always been sure they would turn out to be too much for him to live up to. I have read them, and they are good—cold-blooded and objective, with no trace of anthropomorphism—but too modest in their aim to be intimidating. The sad thing is that N's father has never been very well known outside his own field (I had never heard of him before I met N, for instance); N just thought he was. Even now he mentions his father's name reluctantly to strangers, not wanting to seem to be boasting.

"What did she say your name was?" I remember asking him at Mrs. Sears's nonalcoholic cocktail party, when she had introduced us and left us alone. N was silent, staring at the floor. I looked down to find out what he was looking at, but all I could see was an Oriental rug.

Then he glared at me. "Nat Craig."

"Oh," I said. It wasn't my fault if my company had been forced on him. He ought to be able to see that.

"Nathaniel Craig, Junior." He said the words

slowly, spacing the syllables out and watching for my reaction. He sounded as if he hated his name.

"Am I supposed to have heard of you?" I couldn't think of any other reason for the way he was acting.

He looked at me carefully, and then he smiled. "No, of course not. But I didn't hear your name either."

So I told him, and after that he was charming. The Junior at the end of his name should have given me a clue, but how was I supposed to guess that he thought his father was famous? After that we discovered that neither of us knew the Searses well at all. We wondered why we had been invited. When we met some of the other people in the room, we found that they didn't seem to know their hosts either. It was the first party of that sort that either of us had been to. "Like the Veneerings!" I said to N, and he began to tell me about his work on Dickens.

July 3

This morning I took out the folder of bits of dialogue and description that are meant to fit into my new *Household* novel. It doesn't look promising. The minister is beginning to get out of hand, and if I don't look out, he'll destroy the outline my editor is so enthusiastic about. I put the folder away and started to think about what to do to the house. The problems there are at least in front of my eyes.

When I agreed to buy this house, I didn't realize how long it would take to do most of the work on it myself. Years, that's what it will take. The flagstones, for instance, are almost all too heavy for me to lift. I can drag most of them into place, but only very slowly. Eventually they'll have to be leveled on sand and then set into cement if I don't want them to rock. I assume I'll be able to mix cement, but I never have. H and I have finished scratching up the walls, and I expect to enjoy mud-plastering when I get down to it, but so far I haven't even found out the formula for the plaster.

Then there is the question of dampness. The base of the walls for about ten inches up is still so wet that I don't see how I can expect the mud plaster to stick. Bronson advises me to dig a trench outside to lead rain water away from the house and into the irrigation ditch in back, but I'm not even sure the water will run in the right direction. It seems possible that Bronson just likes the thought of my digging a trench.

The ceiling isn't finished either. It's a good thing Mr. Romero, the drunken plasterer, hasn't arrived yet, because I'm not ready for him. I imagined it might take about a day to scrub the *vigas* clean and tack up chicken wire between them, but I've been working, off and on, for several weeks now, and the larger room isn't even close to being finished. My arms and shoulders tire too quickly, and I always develop a stiff neck. Why doesn't N come, anyway?

I finally started to work this morning on the only project I can imagine finishing. In K's junk pile under the plum trees are enough used cement blocks to form a retaining wall for a small flagstone terrace in front of the house (the floor of my future *portal*). So far, I've dug a shallow ditch and begun to move the irregular lumps of stuck-together cement blocks into it, end over end. When the outside edge is finished, I can ask Mr. Velasquez to fill it with gravel as a base for the flagstones.

* * *

The Pueblo Indians dance to celebrate the Fourth of July. I could hardly believe this when K told me today. "It's good for the tourist trade," he said. "Besides, they're patriotic." He couldn't understand why I was surprised. Well, they have Christmas and Easter dances; why not Independence Day?

But it isn't only the Indians; the McKinneys are planning a Fourth-of-July picnic at the Lawrence range in the mountains, with fireworks at their house afterwards. I keep thinking of our friends at the college, who will surely be holding a memorial service then, with anti-war speakers and sad music and a reading of the names of dead soldiers. My Eastern friends, in their planning discussions, never seem to suspect that people in the rest of the country might have another view of the war or national holidays. And they are beginning to accept into their lives some things that to most people would seem bizarre. I still have a scary sheet of paper I stole from N's Moral Caucus file once. It is headed Medical Guidelines and gives directions on how to avoid being wounded too seriously during a demonstration:

> Our group is pledged to nonviolence. We have no reason to expect that violence will occur, but if it does, certain preparations and coolness will keep injuries to a minimum. In a crowd situation most injuries occur when people panic and run. This causes the police to overreact and brings the danger of trampling those already injured. The most important rule is therefore KEEP COOL. If leaving an area, WALK SLOWLY. Keep cool yourself and try to calm those around you.
>
> You should have had a tetanus toxoid booster in the past year. You can get tetanus (lockjaw) from puncture wounds; it can be fatal. If you did not get the injection before being injured, see your doctor for a booster shot.

"Since there is a possibility of being knocked unconscious," the third paragraph begins. The rest of the page gives sensible advice about not wearing contact lenses, false teeth, earrings, etc. The different kinds of tear gas are described, with their effects (irritation of the respiratory tract, burning eyes, nausea, vomiting, headaches, asthma attacks) and recommendations for treatment. "If pain or blurred vision persists, see a doctor," the last sentence runs. The back of the page is devoted to legal advice. The tone of the whole thing is practical and nonhysterical. The effect is chilling.

It is all true, and these things have happened during peaceful demonstrations, some of them to people I know. It's a question of geography, I suppose. If Kurt and Bronson lived in Boston, they might appear on the Common on the 4th of July with a Viet Cong flag. Here, they set off rockets at a children's picnic, and if I wear a black armband, I'll have to explain what it's for.

"Aren't you coming tomorrow?" K asked me.

I suppose I am, but I would rather be somewhere else.

July 4

The Lawrence ranch. San Cristobal, on the west side of town up in the mountains. The way I see Colorado in my mind, with steep trails disappearing between trees. Pine and aspen and patches of long, soft green grass. (I must learn to identify more trees and wild flowers.) Cool, weightless air. The Hawks' farmhouse partway up, just as it is in the books. Horses in a corral. The caretaker's medium-sized brown house at the top, a fence in front and a Saint Bernard on a chain, barking. In back, the Lawrence house, quite small. (Kitchen where he bustled around cooking wonderful meals while Frieda lounged on the bed with a cigarette dangling from one corner of her mouth—Brett's prejudiced account.) Small *portal* on the front. Everything surprisingly small. The cabin where Brett slept is tiny, maybe twice as big as my outhouse. These were normal-sized people or a bit larger. How did they manage? No wonder they all quarreled so much. (Topic for a thesis on Lawrence?)

A buffalo like a cave painting on the side of the house, done by a group of Indians in memory of D.H.L. and just there for anyone to see as if it were a Chew Mail Pouch Tobacco sign, not protected from weather or vandals. All this belongs to the University of New Mexico now but doesn't appear to be used much. A poet in residence this summer, not home.

The shrine is a tiny building with a window made from a wagon wheel, glass between the spokes. Guest book with a few famous names and lots of academic ones. Tennessee Williams's name was in it when she first came, H says, and Huxley's. And Lawrence's typewriter and old leather jacket used to be in the shrine. Framed letter from the Customs office on the wall, confirming shipment of L's ashes from Vence. His three women had a fight over the ashes before Frieda finally had them mixed in a block of concrete and buried.

The aura is peaceful, beautiful. K and I sat on the steps of the shrine and had white wine and cold chicken while we watched the sun set. Other people sat in quiet, colorful groups, and the children played Statues and made flower chains. No matter what happened afterward, there were no misunderstandings then.

July 5

Katrin was supposed to go with K and me to the picnic yesterday, but she went to a be-in in Trinidad instead, along with the rest of the commune. Kurt explained why she wasn't with him when he picked me up yesterday before the picnic, and I'm sure it's the truth, but I am annoyed with her nevertheless. If she had been there, what happened last night would not have happened, and I might still have a friend.

K's teeth are brownish and crowded in his mouth. Did I notice that before last night? Yes, it was filed away in my mind after I first met him. And could his teeth have had anything to do with the way I treated him?

No. And I'm so sorry it happened. And so angry with him. If he were H, the whole scene would be canceled out by now, for him. But he is not H.

Our conversation in the car on the way down the mountain was usual enough, it seemed to me. Kurt was telling me about a painting he is thinking of doing, of Daphne just before she turned into a laurel tree. "Without leaves or branches or anything," he said, "but she should already be thinking of herself as a tree, and I ought to be able to show that."

I didn't see how he could, except by titling the painting "Daphne," but it was an interesting problem. "What a useful thing to be able to do," I said, "turning into a tree. Almost as good as karate. Imagine the look on his face when she began sprouting leaves."

"It was a dirty trick," he said.

"If you don't mind being a tree for the rest of your life, of course." I was vivacious Anna, chattering on. "The first time I read that story, I thought her father chose a pretty extreme way of protecting her, but now I think it was probably worth it."

"Poor Apollo."

"His own fault. He wasn't in love with her, was he? He couldn't have been." But Apollo probably wouldn't even be in the picture. K almost never paints men, I've noticed.

"Why don't we skip the fireworks?" he said when we reached the main highway. I agreed because I knew that I always turn out to have liked the idea of fireworks much better than the fireworks themselves. I probably would have guessed then what K was thinking if I hadn't been too busy wondering about N. What was N doing yesterday? Something to do with nonviolent civil disobedience, I supposed. Something likely to get him arrested or gassed. The thought of tear gas makes me feel like choking. N is afraid of it too, but that wouldn't stop him from doing whatever he might think was the right thing, whether it had any chance of succeeding or not. I was wishing I knew where he was.

"I shouldn't have gone with you," I said to Kurt. "I shouldn't even be here." And that somehow seemed to me enough of an explanation of what I was thinking, about N and the tear gas and everything else. K's expressive face was partly to blame, I suppose. He always looks so sympathetic that I tend to assume he understands whatever I might be saying to him or even just thinking to myself.

He bumped the car down the road into my yard. "Can I come in for a minute?"

"Yes, please do." He must have seen that I needed company, I thought. We walked up the path together. "Shall I make us some coffee?" I twirled the knob on the stove. We could sit on the couch by the fireplace, and I could talk to him about N and how worried I was. I had tried to confide in H when we were at the ranch, but she immediately misinterpreted what I said, and I hadn't been able to go on. Talking to Kurt would be like telling my problems to a nice, solid adobe wall that wouldn't make judgments or fall down but would just support me if I leaned against it. It would be a relief.

K put his arm around my shoulder then and held on, and I saw what a bad job I must have done of letting him know what I was thinking about in the car. He hadn't communicated very successfully either, and yet there he was, taking it for granted that we were about to make love. Because that was what he had in mind; I could tell by the veiled look in his eyes. "I'll just put the kettle on," I said. Maybe I could tell him about N before it was too late.

It already was, I saw when K put a hand on my other shoulder and turned me to face him. I wouldn't even get a chance to light the stove. "Anna," he said softly, and my feelings were more complicated than they have been for a long time. I tried to pull away, but he put his arms all the way around me and began to stroke my hair. "Beautiful Anna," he murmured.

I smiled at him in a way I hoped was not inviting. "I must warn you that I'm about to turn into a laurel tree, and then won't you be surprised." I tried to step back.

"Beautiful, mysterious Anna."

That was enough. "Stop it," I said, and struggled harder. "Kurt, don't be silly." I could smell kerosene from the stove. I moved sideways and stumbled over Kurt's boot, then cracked my ankle on the end of a rocker. The pain was so sharp that I gasped, and Kurt let go of me.

"What's the matter?" he asked.

I limped away from him and sat in the rocking chair. "It isn't fair," I said. "I thought we were friends."

He smiled in an insinuating way I associate with several other men I have known but never with him. "We are," he said and moved closer. "Beautiful Anna." He looked down at me between swollen eyelids, not seeing me.

"And so we can't just talk?" I was angrier than I had been for a long time. "All the Victorian ideas are still true? I can't invite you into my house at night just to have coffee without you and everybody else assuming that what I really mean is that I want to sleep with you?"

"Oh, come on, Anna. You know what you want as well as I do. Stop pretending."

"I'm not pretending." I was almost crying with rage and disappointment, and I stood up and held my head steady so the tears wouldn't brim out of my eyes. "Just because you want something, does that mean I have to want it too? I thought we were friends," I said again. "I thought you were different." He took a deep breath through his nose and looked grim. Oh no, I thought, now his silly pride is hurt. "Don't you see that men can have it both ways?" He took another breath and opened his mouth, but I went on. "Women too, probably, but that isn't what I'm talking about. If I don't let you visit me alone and I make it obvious that I think you have sex in mind, you can accuse me of being suspicious. And if I do invite you in, it's supposed to mean I'm giving my consent. After that, if I don't give in, I've been leading you on. It isn't fair."

He looked past me at the painting of the red-haired woman with the children. "You're like her, aren't you?" he said. "Just like her. Just as cold." His voice was matter-of-fact, but he was looking at the picture as if he wanted to destroy it.

"And have you forgotten," I said, "that I'm married?"

"Oh, Anna." He looked at me. "Who's being Victorian now? Do you really think you have to be *that* loyal to your husband, even when you know he's sleeping around?"

"Nat? What do you mean? Of course he isn't." I would never have believed before then that I could actually hate Kurt.

"Oh, come off it. What do you think he's been doing all this time?"

I knew that if I tried to answer, my voice would not be reliable. I shook my head from side to side, and the tears fell out of my eyes and began to trail down my face. In a minute my nose would start running, and the box of Kleenex was in the other room.

"Well, good night." He went out the door, and I heard his car starting.

I spun the stove handle closed and got into bed to read myself to sleep with *Emma*. Unluckily, I had just come to the chapter that dealt with Mr. Elton's proposal. Customs may have changed since Emma's day, but people are still misunderstanding each other in ways that aren't very different. I couldn't help feeling as if Kurt were reading the book over my shoulder, pointing out resemblances between my behavior and Emma's, and I wanted to protest the injustice of the comparison.

I had led K on, I was thinking, but I still didn't see how I could have realized it. He has so many women friends, for one thing. H has told me so much about K's various wives and mistresses, past and present, that I have assumed he was well supplied with them and wanted nothing from me but friendship. Surely his relations with Gretchen and H are platonic, and I thought I was in the same category.

I switched to Emerson, hoping for comforting general truths, but even there I kept coming across passages that seemed to have a personal application. "A man may play the fool in the drifts of a desert, but every grain of sand shall seem to see." How did he know I was in a desert?

July 6

The woman in K's painting must be an ex-wife. The Countess, maybe. And are those his children? I have tried to look at the picture with new eyes, but I'm too used to it to see it differently. It's just a picture that I like.

I'm not sure why I took so long to mention N in my quarrel with K, except that my commitment to N seemed too obvious a thing to have to point out. But to K, apparently, it wasn't. I still feel anger when I think of his easy assumption about N, whom he has never met. I wonder what K thought we would do about birth control. I stopped taking pills when I left home and don't have anything else and couldn't bear to imagine having to explain this to him. My having even considered this problem means, perhaps, that I am not so steadfast as I supposed. On the other hand, the fact that I haven't taken the pills since I left N must mean something too.

My behavior towards K hasn't been entirely pure. I can't claim never to have thought of him, smugly, as a conquest. And I have used him, besides, to educate myself. I know quite well that in becoming his friend I was trying, as usual, to enlarge my experience with people and make myself a bit better at dealing with life. And a bit more truthful in writing about it? Yes, I'm afraid so. In spite of my dismay when I realized what K expected the other night, I was tempted briefly to go through with the experience just so I could find out what it was like. Good, I remember thinking with part of my mind, it's happening at last. The number of adultery scenes in novels has been puzzling me. Do the authors write entirely from imagination? In some cases it certainly doesn't seem that way, but perhaps real writers don't work the way I do. I am sure only that if I ever attempted to write such a scene without some kind of experience to base it on, it would turn out to be not just falsely fashionable, but unbelievable. I would be like my mother at H's wedding, wearing lipstick for the first time in her life and getting it on her teeth.

Reason took over very quickly after that thought, and I saw that the idea of using K as source material hadn't been serious. It was only the basis for an anecdote to be told against myself to some unidentified friend, probably N.

K likes to think he knows people to the depths of

their souls. It's a good thing he doesn't. He looks intently into their eyes and nods to himself. With him, I project a personality I don't use on anyone else, and he picks it up and thinks he understands me.

July 8

Buy weed cutter! The light that comes through my big window is greener every day. Some kind of huge, triffid-like plant has suddenly appeared by the dozen and sneaks closer when I'm not looking.

Why is the yard full of dangerous junk? Most of it doesn't show from a distance, but the ground under the garlic and mint and all the other green, fragrant things is covered with rusty hardware and pieces of old bottles. The trouble with all this trash is that it distracts me from the big jobs. When the sun shines at a certain angle, it catches the curved edges of the broken glass and the whole yard glitters. Then, if I'm feeling weak minded, I can waste hours walking around with a coffee can, picking up shards.

July 9

Mexican tiles as a baseboard, set into cement? To solve the dampness problem. Might work. Investigate.

July 10

Cement tiles, H says they're called. A foot square, in a variety of colors. Can be bought in Santa Fe. I hadn't seen her (or anyone else, practically) for nearly a week and thought I ought to. Cowardly or prudent, I checked to see whose car might be parked in front of her house, saw no one's, and dared to stop, finding only Gretchen there visiting. She walks across the fields with her cross-eyed children trailing after, gathering flowers. She's the only adult in town who walks anywhere (except my mailbox thief). She and H were having one of those obstetrical conversations that I can't bear (pun?) because other people are so conscious of my being left out.

Gretchen: "It is funny; the first time, I never thought about my baby. I thought only that I would be pregnant and I would go to the hospital and then I would not be pregnant."

It was H who brought the subject up. How can she be interested still, after seven years?

They started out by discussing Katrin, her insisting on having her baby at home, alone. Gretchen: "I think she is brave. Would you do that?"

H, surprisingly cynical: "She says she did it. How do we know she really did?"

I, cold reason as usual: "If she wasn't afraid, she wasn't brave."

H: "Well, she should have been afraid. If she had known what she was doing."

"Do you suppose her name is really Katrin?" I asked, to change the direction of the conversation.

"Why shouldn't it be?" But H was intrigued.

"Look who introduced her. Does Kurt ever get anybody's name right?" I said. "I'll bet ten cents her name is really Katherine."

Or was I trying to get them to talk about K, to see if he had said anything about me? I suppose I was. If so, I failed. They were just on the verge of admitting, finally, how they felt about Katrin, and they wouldn't be diverted. She never wears shoes, Gretchen told us, because they're bad for the circulation. "Do we wear shoes on our hands?" she asked Gretchen. And she doesn't believe in doctors or birth control or anything else unnatural.

"She's a refugee, isn't she? I heard she was born in a country that doesn't even exist anymore," H said, pretending to defend her. "That's why she talks in stage diction, because English isn't her native language."

And then I made some reference to Katrin's "throaty laugh." The others seized on it delightedly and welcomed me to the conversation, and I couldn't resist going on. "And the way she throws her head back." I threw my head back. I am as accurate a mimic as H when I can forget that imitating people isn't nice.

"Yes, yes." (Gretchen) "You have it exactly. So false, is it not?" And then paused, looking at us to see if she had gone too far. But we were all laughing now and competing with each other in imitations of Katrin's mannerisms. It was the first time we realized we shared a common feeling about Katrin; we were so used to hearing her praised.

I: "That reverent tone whenever she says 'Nature.'"

"Yes, yes, and she says it so often!" H gasped.

"More often than Father does, do you think?"

"Oh, twice as much! He gives some of the credit to God, but with Katrin it's always Nature. Invariably."

I, suddenly: "Why do we all hate her so much?"

"Oh, we don't hate her." H paused. "Well, yes, we do."

Is Katrin so different from the rest of us? She cooks, sews, cleans, sings, and feeds her baby, but so do most of the other women here. The difference is, I think, not that she does these things, but that she makes a show, sincerely or not, of enjoying them. She is someone that we all have been told we ought to be—but that we don't necessarily want to be for the rest of our lives. She is our enemy.

4

July 14

Two separate letters from my parents, in the same envelope. Father's is brief, loving, formal. He hopes I am well and exclaims over the beauty of the seashore, mentions Nature's bounty. Mother, assuming I see H every day, writes a joint letter to both of us. She imagines us having "wonderful family fun." But my father frets about his former church, she says. The new young minister with the obligatory beard has quickly captivated his congregation because he watches the same television programs they do and begins every sermon with three jokes. He hasn't even tried to charm my mother, who reports his failure to invite my father, the Minister Emeritus, to a ceremony honoring the new carillon.

H was working in the kitchen when I took Mother's letter to her. We discussed Father for a while without discovering anything new except that more of our childhood memories differ. H wasn't looking well. The inside corners of her eye sockets were dark and bruised-looking, and she sighed between sentences. Either she was sick, I thought, or she had been fighting with Seth.

"Are you well?" I asked her. I hoped it wasn't a fight.

"Oh, fine," she said, and sighed. "I suppose it's funny, really." Seth frightened her today, without meaning to and without even knowing it, apparently. She and Seth had been arguing, she told me, when he suddenly stalked out of the house and went to his studio. "As usual," H said. But then, about fifteen minutes later, when she was sprinkling water on the kitchen floor and starting to sweep it, she heard a shot from the direction of the studio. As soon as she could move, she ran outside and flung open Seth's door, too terrified even to stop and think of what she might find. Seth was leaning out of the window opposite the doorway. She could see only his legs and the seat of his pants, which, she says, needed a new patch. He straightened up and faced her, and she saw a pistol dangling from his hand. "Got 'im," he said.

He had shot a snake from the window, at very short range. A rattlesnake? All that was left was a mess of blood and scaly stripes. Later, H found Tomas crying. "It was only a grass snake," he said. "I know it was. Why did he have to kill it?" H hadn't known that Seth had a gun or knew how to use one. She wouldn't say, even to me, what she had thought when she heard the shot.

Afterwards she started talking about the Playhouse, explaining to me why she had left. "I just couldn't stay there and do all the things you have to do if you're an actress. It wasn't a question of having to sleep with the director or anything like that. At least . . ." She was sifting flour and salt into a big blue pottery bowl. "But you had to keep pushing yourself all the time—push, push, push. It's hard to believe in yourself that much."

It made me sad. I've always thought she did believe in herself. Even when she cooks, she does it with so much confidence that I love to watch her. "But you've done acting here, haven't you?" I asked her.

"Melodramas with the local amateur group. Three highschool girls, every homosexual in town, all the local doctors, a few businessmen's wives bored with the garden club, and one real-estate man who recites dialect monologues. You can always get a cast for *The Drunkard,* but if you mention Chekhov, everybody groans."

It sounded like Chekhov, I thought. Frustrated provincial wives and doctors. I didn't see why she couldn't get them to do *The Seagull.*

She slumped at the table. "You don't know those idiots. Everybody's late for rehearsals, and they ham their parts and put in new lines with local jokes. Maybe I'll take up weaving after all. At least it's something you can do alone."

Before I left, she apologized for being in a bad mood. "I'm Harriet Gloom today, I guess." The veins that branch down into the top of her blouse looked navy blue this morning, and her ribs were more distinct than before. I didn't see how she could stand her life.

July 15

At least some of her memories are like mine. Harriet Gloom and Anne Despair. The game we invented after reading *Pollyanna.* Each of us trying to think of as many things as possible to complain about. Our parents didn't approve but used it against us for years afterwards. "I see we have Miss Gloom with us this evening," Mother would say brightly if adolescent H sulked at the dinner table.

Does H think of Mother's life when she contemplates her own? We could never seriously believe that our mother had once had ambitions to become a professional lieder singer or that she had been a Young Socialist, and we would not have thought of relating these facts to our own future.

Mother used to embarrass us so often. When she wore her Girl Scout leader uniform to church, for instance. (We were proud of that when we were small but soon got over it.) And then later there were other things. She has never known much about how people actually talk. (She still refers to our friends as "chums," in quotation marks, as if she were quoting us.) That time when Melisande was a baby and H was showing her off to a roomful of Alliance ladies. Melisande crawled in an unusual, twisty way, dragging herself across the floor on her stomach and alternate forearms, and Mother was enchanted. "Look at her screwing around!" she exclaimed.

Both my parents have that same terrible innocence. It's the quality H and I have most dreaded to find in ourselves, and yet, of course, neither of us could really escape it. Would it have helped if our brother had been born alive? My big brother and H's little one. Thomas, his name was to have been.

I must stop letting N and H and my own doubts distract me from the new *Household* novel. Once I get started, I should be able to work on it every morning and have it finished by the end of the summer. The other one took only six weeks, after all.

July 17

Very strange, what happened last night. I was sitting at the kitchen table trying, and failing, to write a letter to N. He should be here by now if he is coming at all, and so I suppose he isn't coming. I didn't know what to say to him. I felt quite isolated, as I always do here at night. From the windows I could see the light of occasional cars, interrupted by trees, passing along Ranchitos Road just across the river, but there was no sign of the existence of other people nearby. All sorts of quarrels, orgies, or fiestas could go on behind the thick adobe walls here without anyone's neighbors suspecting anything at all. Some of the men go out in the evenings—I know Luis Ortega does, for instance—but I seldom hear them. Even the tavern on the corner isn't a source of much light or noise; people just drive up to it and go inside. I sometimes hear from Angie or from the local radio station about fights that have occurred there, but if I didn't know where the tavern was, I don't think I could guess.

I looked up from my writing and saw the headlights of a car approaching. Luis, no doubt, coming back from the bar. But the lights wavered down the road, disappeared behind trees, appeared again, and stopped at my fence. I am ashamed to remember how panic-stricken I was. I felt like a rabbit, caught between an impulse to run into the other room and an even stronger one to flatten myself against the door where I wouldn't be seen from the windows. I wished I had curtains, at least, and on a mental list I wrote: "Have porch light installed."

Footsteps approached, running through the weeds toward the house. The headlights were still on, down by the fence. "Nat?" I called, so softly that no one could have heard me.

There was a series of knocks on the door, and H's voice came, excited and impatient. "Anne, open the door!" My hand felt weak as I slid the bolt out of its socket and turned the knob. H stood on the doorstep looking ecstatic. Her head was thrown back, and her golden eyes shone. "I'm free," she almost sang. "I told him I was leaving, and I left." Behind her, the headlights turned and vanished.

"How did you get here?" I think I still thought she was N.

"I hitchhiked." Her eyes had a mischievous glitter. "Not with a stranger. I can stay with you, can't I? You don't mind? I can sleep on the couch and help with the mud-plastering."

"I don't mind. But what about the children?"

"He'll take care of the children. He's scared. I've never seen him scared before." She smiled at me, looking sideways. "I guess running away must be a family trait."

"But what did he do? Why?" I wasn't sure I could stand to hear all about what Seth had done this time, but H would tell me anyway. It must be something pretty bad.

Her face took on a set, hard look suddenly, and she marched into the living room. "Why don't you start a fire?" She sat on the couch and put her raffia bag down beside her. It was stuffed with clothes, I saw. "I didn't bring much," H said. "I figured I could borrow things from your vast wardrobe."

"What did he do?" I asked her again. She didn't have a black eye or a swollen lip, and if Seth had hurt any of the children, she wouldn't have left them with him.

"Oh, nothing. He gave away a painting." H paused, and her eyes had big, dramatic pupils. "To Katrin."

This must be worse than it sounded. "How vile," I felt I was expected to say. I saw signs that H was about to begin crying, and I wished desperately that I could think of some way to prevent her.

"You don't understand, do you?" H gasped out her words and started rummaging through her bag. "You don't know Seth. He has never, in his whole life, given anything to anybody and yet there he was giving Katrin one of his best paintings. *Presenting* it to her."

"Well, why?"

"Because she admired it." She found a Kleenex and blew her nose. "Never. Even Christmas presents. The children and I make them for each other and pretend they're from him. We're used to it. We don't expect anything different. But that doesn't mean he has any right." She pounded on the couch with her fist.

"How did it happen?"

"And it was my painting. Oh, he never actually said so, but he didn't object when I hung it in the kitchen. That was a long time ago, and we've always referred to it as my picture. At least I have. I loved that picture."

"Did Katrin know it was yours? I bet she'd give it back if she knew."

" 'But that's mine,' I said when I saw him actually start to take it down from the wall. Nobody heard me. It was as if I weren't even there. Seth was working all day on the crate for the big painting for the Dallas show, and Katrin and Kurt came over with Ben Wickersham, that art critic. You should have heard Seth showing off, talking about 'plastic values' or something of the sort. Then Katrin started admiring his work in a way that implied that I didn't have the brains to admire it. I can't explain what I mean. She was doing it on purpose, very calculatingly, and yet I was the only one who saw through her."

"And so he gave her your painting."

"She *loved* the one he was sending to Dallas. 'Do you want it?' he asked her. The painting he's been working on for six months and expects to win a prize before some Texas millionnaire buys it for a museum. Even Kurt was startled, and naturally Katrin refused. 'Well, take this one then,' said the reckless, lavish genius, and reached up to the wall for my painting." H was throwing herself into the scene and seemed almost amused.

"The one with the hinges," I said.

"What hinges?" She looked briefly offended. "Little metal wings. That's the way I thought of them. You don't know how I loved them. That's when I said 'That's mine,' and my voice came out squeaky and too thin to be heard."

"You couldn't help feeling that you were being petty."

"Exactly. I almost apologized. But I couldn't just not say anything." Her head drooped. "Of course Katrin would give it back if I asked her, but you know how she would make me feel."

"Yes."

"Like some worm. And I would hate that painting so much by then, I would never want to see it again. I already do hate it, as a matter of fact. As far as I'm concerned, it's ruined." She sighed. "Like everything else in my life."

My beautiful sister has come back. That was all I could think when I saw her in the doorway, and yet I was dismayed and I felt sure she had done the wrong thing. I suppose she will stay here for a few days and then go home, though she says not. I can just barely believe that she might leave S, but I know she wouldn't abandon her children.

She looked happy last night, and very young. Not hysterical. The little dents were gone from the skin around her eyes. "This is the first time in fourteen years that I've done what I wanted to do," she said to me.

July 18

H isn't angry with Seth any more, but I don't think she has any plans yet for going back to him. When she told me about his giving away the painting, I understood how she felt, and yet I was almost charmed because her story showed something about him that I hadn't known—not generosity, but a human susceptibility to flattery I wouldn't have suspected him of possessing.

It isn't going to be easy for us to live so close together. "Two of us, both running away at once," H said yesterday, smiling at me over her fourth piece of whole-wheat toast with lime marmalade. "It's ridiculous. As if we had both sprained our right ankles at the same time, or broken our noses. We should avoid being seen together." Her eyes sparkled yellow-green like the marmalade, and her hair caught gleams from the strong sunlight in the kitchen.

"It isn't the same. I didn't run away." I retreated to the next room and got out my materials for scrubbing the *vigas*.

She followed me, still in her nightgown. "Why do you insist on washing your *vigas*, anyway?" She was standing next to the chest of drawers, and she reached for my hairbrush.

"Because Kurt started to do it last year, and the clean places show up the rest." I stopped myself from asking whether H hadn't brought her own brush, but I couldn't help the direction my eyes took.

She saw me in the mirror and paused with her hand on the brush. "What's the matter? Do you have some disease of the scalp?"

"No, of course not. Go ahead." Why can't I ever simply mind something my sister does without feeling that the fault is really my own?

Later I stood on the ladder and scrubbed the *vigas* while H handed me cleaning supplies and explained her real reason for leaving Seth.

"It wasn't because he gave away my painting," she said. "Well, it was, but really it was because of something he said earlier in the same conversation. He referred to himself as a New Mexico artist. He talked as if we expected to stay here all our lives." She paused dramatically, staring up at me.

"Don't you?" I was surprised.

"Plan to stay here forever? What do you mean? It was supposed to be only temporary, just till Seth got established as an artist." She sat down on the couch away from my dripping sponge. "All these years I've been so patient, not pushing him into making definite plans. But he can't pretend not to have known I was expecting to leave. 'When we go back East,' both of us used to say, all the time. Now he claims we always intended to stay here. Where else could he find such good working conditions, with free housing and plenty of time? That's what he asked last night, and I didn't know any way to answer him. He doesn't even see what it's doing to the children. He claims it's good for them to live this way."

"Maybe in some ways it is." But I couldn't think of any just then.

"With no permanent home? Always having to be outsiders, never fitting in with the other children? Do you know that Tomas thinks there's something wrong with his hair, just because it isn't black? He used to cry about it. Do you want to know what my secret dream for them is? A split-level house in New Jersey with a little square lawn in front and a big square lawn in back. Elm trees and sidewalks and dogs on leashes."

I couldn't tell how serious she was. "Do you think any of you would fit in there?"

"Seth with an attaché case and one of those little hats, and me having to collect for the United Fund? No, I can't quite see it. But this kind of life isn't right for us either. There are altogether too many peculiar people here, for one thing."

I sat down on the top of the ladder. The water in my bucket was black already, and the sponge had begun to make streaks. "Not everybody peculiar is here. I don't know whether people in the East are unhappier than they were when you lived there, but it shows more than it used to. And the elm trees are dying.

Don't you remember how out of place we felt growing up in neighborhoods like the one you describe? More people feel that way now, but that doesn't make it any better."

"Maple, then. You don't know what I would give for one good, solid, messy maple tree," H said. "Seth always said he was going to go into teaching. He still gets offers. All right, we might meet unhappy people, but they couldn't all be as unstable as the ones who drift in and out of here."

That was true, I thought.

"It was one night last summer that I really started thinking about it. We had a painter staying with us for a while. Jerome. He did the blue portrait of me, the one by our fireplace."

I thought of the living room of the Huggins house, where there are five portraits of H, in five different styles.

"He used to get drunk every night in a nice, quiet way," she said. "The children didn't even seem to notice. He would sing for them sometimes, and trade riddles, and they loved having him here. But one night when he had been with us for about a week, we went out to a party and Jerome went to the Inn with some friends. We came back about midnight and Melisande met us at the door in her nightgown, looking very grown-up and confidential. 'Ssh,' she said. 'I've just gotten Jerome settled. He was too drunk to put himself to bed, but we managed.' "

I misunderstood. "Had he hurt her?"

H stared. "Jerome? What do you mean? No, but it was so sad the way she took the whole thing for granted. She had led him into his bedroom and taken his shoes off, and then she had found a blanket to cover him. Just as if he were Tomas. She managed so well. That was what upset me, her accepting the whole thing as a part of ordinary life. What would we have done at her age if a drunken friend of Father's had staggered into the parsonage in the middle of the night when nobody else was home?"

I tried to imagine Father with that kind of friend. "Sneaked out the back door and spent the night in the tree house, I suppose."

"Something like that. But not Melly. Seth was proud of her. I was too, in a way."

Seth didn't come to see H yesterday, and by this afternoon we were beginning to wonder whether he was going to come at all. "Not that I want him to," she said, "but I just thought he might."

"Maybe he doesn't know where you are."

"He knows," H said.

It was Bronson who finally came, when H and I were in the kitchen discussing our plans for further work on the house. I had just finished scrubbing the *vigas* and was wondering whether I ought to tack up the rest of the chicken wire. If I tried to do it today, I feared my neck would be so stiff that I wouldn't be able to look down for a week. Then I glanced out the window and saw a jeep stop at the end of my lot near the fence. "It's Bronson!" H said, looking over my shoulder, and Bronson's tall, stooped figure climbed out and sauntered toward the house.

H ran away into the living room as I went to the door to let him in.

"You must be pleased," Bronson said to me.

"What? No. Why should I be?" So he had come from Seth.

His eyes searched the kitchen and focused, narrowing, on me as he propped himself against the wall next to the door. "This is what you had in mind all along, isn't it—for Harriet to leave Seth?"

I don't know why I still react every time Bronson insults me. I should be used to him by now. "No, it isn't," I said, and a pain gripped my right shoulder. It was hard to look up at him. Bronson always holds his head on one side when he talks to me, and the cramp in my neck was making me seem to be imitating him. I was afraid he would demand to see H, and I wondered how I was going to get rid of him.

Then H appeared in the living-room doorway with a look of surprise on her face. "Bronson!"

He transferred his gaze to her. I murmured something about having to buy chicken wire and plunged past H into the other room to get my wallet and car keys. When I came back through the kitchen, neither of them had moved. Bronson still had a haughty, accusing expression, and H was looking at the floor. "Good-bye, Sister Anne," Bronson said softly as I passed him.

"Good-bye." I tried not to hurry to the car, though I knew the others wouldn't be watching anyway. Poor H.

I wanted to go to the grocery store or the library, but I was afraid of meeting someone I knew, and I didn't want to have to talk about H (or, even worse, *not* talk about H) until the situation was clearer. I have been avoiding Kurt ever since the night of the picnic, and now it seems I have to avoid everyone else too. The Post Office wouldn't do either, though I would have liked to check my mailbox. Finally I settled for going to Pilar, a tiny village down the highway near the Gorge, to dig the sand I need for the plastering. I had to work slowly because of my sore shoulder, but that was just as well. I dawdled purposely, taking several hours to fill five grocery boxes with sand. Then I drove home by the back way along the river, admiring the mellow afternoon light on meadows, horses, and low, flat houses. New Mexico is more beautiful than the South of France. But who was Sister Annie? The evil sister in a fairy tale.

I could see as I drove down Ranchitos Road that Bronson's jeep was gone, and I came into the house to find my sister sitting by the empty fireplace, looking at the sunset framed in the big window.

"He was trying to talk me into going back to Seth," H said. She wasn't crying, at least. "I suppose Seth was too busy to come himself. He's still trying to get the big painting ready in time for the Dallas show. First things first." She made a solemn Seth face.

"He's probably afraid that if he comes, the fight will start all over again."

"Exactly. And so he sends his best friend. Seth hates to argue with me because I always win. Not that it does me any good, because when he can't think of anything more to say, he goes out to his studio and bolts the door. But that wouldn't work this time. He must have been hoping Bronson would make me see reason without any trouble at all."

"Did Seth really send him?"

"I don't know. Bronson did tell him he was coming." She laughed. "They're worried about food, it seems. Gretchen sent over a stew last night, but she can't keep on doing that. Bronson was trying to make me feel sorry for Gretchen. Well, I am sorry, but I don't think there's anything I can do about it. I can't cook anymore; I just can't. The very thought of trying just one more time to decide what we'll all eat next sends me into a panic. That's almost all I've done for the last fourteen years, it seems to me, and I can't take it any longer. I'm just not strong enough. I *can't* cook." Her eyes filled with tears.

"I know." I hoped I didn't sound ironic. I've already noticed that H has given up cooking. She can't wash dishes either, apparently, or make beds.

July 19

"Sister Anne, do you see anyone coming?" The sister who spoils the story by asking questions, making the heroine see her marriage from the outside. But Anne was Bluebeard's sister-in-law—I remember now—and even Bronson couldn't say she was wrong to interfere. ("I see nothing but a dust, and the grass, which looks green," I think she answered, looking desperately out of the tower for help.)

Can it be my fault? Has H left S because of me? "Why do you stay with him, then?" I think I asked after one of her complaints. "I wouldn't." "No, I can see you wouldn't," she said, and looked at me. But H would never do anything just because I told her to. Would she? She and I have always been jealous of each other, wanting what the other has without really understanding what it is:

1. She thinks of me as having a successful career.

2. I have no children and appear to have left my husband.

Put it another way: Would H have run away if I hadn't come here? Probably not. I wouldn't have been here for her to run to, for one thing. (Or would Cornelia or Gretchen or anyone else have done just as well?) But I think she probably didn't complain as much before she began to tell me about her marriage, and therefore didn't examine her life. Perhaps she was even happy, or thought she was.

My triffids are sunflowers. H could hardly believe my ignorance when I asked about them. I should have known. A few are even beginning to bloom. Still, there are more than my yard needs.

I got out the notes for my novel today and looked them over, regretting H's timing. I had planned to begin writing this week, and her being here was bound to be a distraction, I thought.

I read the notes over anyway, just to see whether I could do anything with them. To my dismay, I see that I can't. And the reasons have nothing to do with H. The whole thing is simply all wrong. In the first place, the quarrel scene, when the minister's wife refuses to go to church, won't do. And the minister himself is becoming a prig who can't possibly win sympathy, much less arouse the necessary sexy feelings. Maybe if I made him a little bit like Bronson? Religious but too personal at the same time? That might do it.

The problem is that I have material for a real novel, but what I am supposed to write is an unreal one.

Can I simply follow the material where it wants to go and then pare the whole thing down to a *Household* novel afterwards? I don't think so. I am breaking too many rules.

For one thing, I am beginning not to believe in endings, happy or otherwise. I'm not even sure I can write one. And I do believe in meaningless coincidence and am not certain it should be excluded from fiction.

My editor will never put up with such notions. Quite right, too. Dr. Peck's report (reward score −40) on the book as I see it: "*Passion under the Cross* (or whatever title it might have by the time it ends up in the magazine) was the most unrewarding novel published by *Household* in fifteen years. Most of the readers who began it were unable to finish more than a few paragraphs, and those who read further felt threatened and confused by the absence of a familiar, comforting solution to the problems of its characters. 'Everything was left all up in the air,' was the typical response of a thirty-eight-year-old mother of three, wife of a garage mechanic: 'The way those people were acting was just crazy, and it wasn't realistic. At first I liked the young minister, but then when he gave that political sermon and half the choir walked out, I couldn't look up to him anymore, and it was downhill from there on. Very poor, I thought.' " etc.

So what do I do with these notes? The plot is a good, standard *Household* plot. Any story written around it should tug at the heartstrings: +70 at least. But I can't write it. I could have, probably, if I had gone ahead last fall, when I had just the outline and a very shallow notion of the characters. But I was distracted then, by sickness and the election and other events, and that's when I started to take all these notes. I thought about my characters while I was doing other things. Passages of description or dialogue would come to me, and I would write them down. The people became complex, and now they won't fit into my outline.

H and I may as well try to finish the house.

July 20

Kurt arrived this morning, bringing two buckets filled with lumps of fine, cream-colored clay called *tierra bayeta* for plastering the walls. He didn't seem surprised to see H; in fact, he was so formal and self-conscious that I am convinced he wouldn't have come at all if he hadn't counted on the presence of a third person. ("I suppose everyone knows I'm here," H said later. "It will be in the society column of next week's paper. 'Harriet Huggins of Arroyo Seco is visiting the gracious Ranchitos home of her sister, Anne Craig.' ")

"I told you I'd help you finish the house, Anna," Kurt said, while H looked curiously from him to me. "Did you think I wouldn't?"

"No, of course not." But of course I had.

He inspected the ceiling and promised to try again to get it plastered. Mr. Romero has definitely been on the way to the house at least twice to K's knowledge. "Too bad you live so near the bar. He starts out for your house and gets distracted." He smiled with one side of his mouth and then looked grim, staring at me. I felt terrible.

I was afraid of H's questions after K had left, but she attributed his stiffness to her own situation. "I suppose he's on Seth's side," she said, "like everyone else. Somehow, I thought Kurt would be different." Guiltily, I failed to explain.

We spent the rest of the day mixing plaster—three parts sand to one part dirt, enough water to make a paste, and as much straw as the mixture will hold—and starting on the walls. H had somehow found out Bronson's formula, said to be the best in town. The soft plaster reminds me of coconut frosting. I was frustrated at first to find that most of it tended to slide off the wall and fall in sugary masses at the foot of the ladder. Later I discovered that by wetting down the wall underneath and putting enough pressure on the plaster as I smoothed it on, I could make it stay. It's slow work, but we've finished the chimney and fireplace and most of the window wall so far.

Angie Ortega came over to marvel at the crazy Anglos doing work that they should have paid Indian women to do. Like Kurt, she was unsurprised to find H living here.

H is beginning to miss her children. She burst into tears today at the sight of the glue container on my kitchen shelf. "Bad Cow Glue," she sobbed. "That's what Tomas used to call it when he was little, because of the picture on the bottle. 'That's nice Elmer,' I told him, but he said, 'No, he looks mean. He's a bad cow.' And it's true. Have you ever looked at that picture?"

Later in the afternoon she was wearing my red kimono and lying on the couch we had pushed across the room, out of the way of the falling plaster. "It isn't that I'm really worried about them. They're old enough to get their own meals if they have to, and they've always been good at entertaining themselves, but I'm so afraid of what they must be thinking." She was directly under the painting of Kurt's wife and children, as if some cunning movie director had placed her there to give emphasis to what she was saying. "They'll think I've left *them,* not Seth. They're bound to. I didn't have time to explain to them. How did Frieda stand it, anyway?" H read herself to sleep last night with *Not I but the Wind . . .*, and all day she kept pointing out parallels between Frieda Lawrence's situation and her own.

"Wouldn't Seth have thought of some explanation to give them? I don't think he's purposely cruel, is he?"

"No," she moaned, "not to them."

"Or Gretchen, when she brought their supper. She would have told them that you're sick or tired out or something and you're just staying here till you feel better. I know she would."

"Oh, I'm such a terrible mother. I've never been any good at it, really."

"Well, who is?" My container of plaster was empty, and I climbed down the ladder to refill it.

"Even at breast-feeding I was a failure." H was gazing up at the painting, as if it were some ideal that she could never live up to.

"Oh, no, surely not. I remember . . ."

"That was a fake. I didn't want people to know, but I almost always had to give a supplementary bottle!" she wailed.

I was embarrassed. I climbed the ladder again and smeared on another handful of mud.

"And I started them on solid foods as soon as I could." H drooped across the couch, graceful and defeated. "A complete failure."

July 22
Santa Fe—The Blue Door Motel

Going to the opera alone. A year ago it wouldn't

have occurred to me to do anything so adventurous. But H didn't feel like coming—is clearly waiting for S to come and talk her into going back to him. And someone had to buy the supplies I need for finishing the room. H was happy to get rid of me for a while—must be as strained by all this proximity as I am. She promised to let Mr. Romero in and supervise the ceiling work. (I don't believe he exists but do hope he came.)

White cement tiles about ten inches square to form a baseboard. I got two with blue doves on them to put on each side of the doorway, two more for the base of the fireplace. Also bedspreads, blue Mexican glasses, and a few other things. A handwoven tie for Father, and one for N. The car is weighed down with the tiles and makes more noise than ever. The way it looks is bad enough, with all those dents put into it by N's students backing it into parking meters, but it sounds even worse. I don't trust it, am glad I decided in advance to spend the night here and drive back in the morning.

My favorite sign in this area, advertising one of those pools that are stocked with trout for tourists: "Enjoy the Thrill of Catching Fighting Mountain Trout—the Easy Way!" I may send a picture of it to N's father.

Chili rellenos for supper, with *sopapillas* and honey.

The Marriage of Figaro. So much artifice and civilization set down intact in that small enclosure in the wilderness. Like walking through the canyon and finding a Viennese petit-point brooch half-hidden by layers of old fallen pine needles. Clear voices coming in patterns across the pool of water in front of the stage. The most sophisticated audience I have seen in this country, full of wise international faces I felt I ought to recognize. And all bundled up against the cold in various elegant wraps and stoles. Even the ushers wore serapes and long, warm skirts.

Perhaps by the time I get back tomorrow Seth will have persuaded H to return. I don't know what else she can do, really. Maybe he'll agree at least to think about moving to Albuquerque or Santa Fe, where there are theatres H could work in. That's all she wants, she says.

July 23

A mystery today that disturbs me more than it probably should. Because the muffler and tailpipe finally dropped off the car, I had to spend the afternoon at a garage in Espanola. The sun was beginning to set by the time I reached my exit from Ranchitos Road. I drove the car, heavy with the unaccustomed weight of the tiles, slowly down the slope and over the bridge. If I could manage to avoid the ruts in the yard, I should be able to get almost to the door. I turned the corner around the clump of lilacs by the river and stopped suddenly; I had nearly driven into a brand-new fence.

It was an extension of the Ortegas' regular fence—two strands of barbed wire and a raw-looking post that sealed off what I have come to think of as my driveway. I know, of course, that the little bit of property between my yard and the river isn't mine, but Luis did invite me to use it to get to my usual parking place. He must have changed his mind.

I backed the car carefully and turned it, avoiding holes and broken glass, and drove a few yards along the river through sunflowers and Queen Anne's lace to the road that is the official entrance to my house. Enough people have used it in the last few months, mostly by mistake, to keep the tallest weeds down, and I was able to drive fairly close to the house. Still, I was puzzled about the Ortegas. I gathered up a few of the packages and went into the house.

H was sitting at the table wearing a lace-trimmed white nightgown and my stole and stirring a cup of mint tea, looking dreamily out the window at the mountains, as if she were waiting for Renoir to paint her. "Hi," she said. "Did you have a good time?" As dutifully as if she were talking to one of her children just back from school, but with her mind somewhere else.

"What happened about the fence?"

"Fence?" She had stopped focusing on the mountains, but her green-yellow eyes still looked lighted.

"The Ortegas. Is something wrong?" The Ortegas might have explained to H, I thought, and she must at least have noticed Luis digging the hole for the post.

She hadn't noticed. "Oh, they're Spanish, you know, and you never can tell. Let's see what you got at the Old Mexico Shop."

"I'll have to ask Angie. They told me to use their driveway."

"I wouldn't ask. I'm sure it wasn't her idea, but she'll have to defend Luis and his famous pride." H unfolded the Indian bedspread I bought today—cream with a red design and a row of blue elephants marching around the border. "Mm. Lovely. Curtains for the big window?"

Angie won't mind my asking, I know, but I still have an unpleasant feeling.

July 24—morning

Right now I feel as if I've spent a large part of my life failing to understand my own sister. I should have known last night that there was something she wasn't telling me.

About an hour ago, when I was sitting at the table with my coffee, I heard Luis come out of the house next door and drive away. It seemed like a good time for me to talk with Angie, and I hoped to find her hanging out the wash or working in the garden. Once she gets in the house, it's hard to get in touch with her, because the noise of television cartoons and game shows drowns out the sound of knocking on the door.

I was in luck. Angie was sweeping her new cement front steps, and I caught her eye and waved to her. "Angie," I called.

She smiled brightly, opened the scrolled aluminum screen door, and started to go inside.

I ran toward her, still waving. She looked quickly toward the end of her driveway and then beckoned me to come inside. "Good morning," she said. "Have you heard about our fireplace? Luis got the bricks yesterday." She pointed to a stack of yellowish-tan glazed bricks in the corner of the room.

I wouldn't have believed there were any bricks like those in New Mexico. They're the kind I associate with rows of 1930 bungalows with arched brick porches on the front. But Luis is determined to make his house as Anglo as possible, and I've almost resigned myself by now to finding, every time I visit the Ortegas, that he's done something new to ruin it. "Well," I said, "it will be nice to have a fire, anyway."

"There won't be a fire." Angie smiled, looking as pretty as ever in spite of the crown of pink plastic curlers in her black hair. "Luis doesn't like open fires. Too dirty."

A fake fireplace. I might have known. It was clear by then that she wasn't going to bring up the subject of the fence. "I just wanted to say," I said uncomfortably, "that I'm sorry if you've minded my using your driveway."

She bent her curler-topped head and sat very still, looking down at her hands.

"I must have misunderstood," I said. "I thought Luis told me to use it."

"He did!" Angie looked at least as distressed as I felt. "He only . . . he might try to grow something on that little piece of land there, you know, or . . ." She gave up.

"Of course." I smiled and started toward the door. "Well, tell him not to worry. I just wondered about the fence."

She followed me, looking even more distressed. "Anne. I'm sorry. But Luis got mad about Bronson."

"Bronson?"

"Yes. Mr. McKinney. You can't blame Luis."

"I don't know what you mean. Was Bronson using the driveway?"

She looked terribly embarrassed. "I mean, I don't think it's our business what your sister does, and that's what I told Luis, but I don't think it was right for Bronson to park on our land all night. That was what made Luis mad. I can't tell you the things he said about Harriet, but he doesn't want me to go to your house anymore while she's there."

"Harriet." I was afraid I was beginning to understand. "I see. I'll talk to her and find out . . . I mean, I'm sure there was some reason . . ."

"Didn't you know? I'm sorry. Oh, I'm sorry."

"Yes, well, good-bye, Angie." I fled out the door and closed it carefully.

When H left Seth, can she have been planning to run away with Bronson? But I don't even know whether he really spent the whole night here or whether it means anything if he did or whether the Ortegas are exaggerating, and I can't think of any other way of finding out besides questioning H, who is conveniently sleeping late. Her life is her own business, but what I mind is her using me, using my house, and not telling me what she was planning to do or had done. She must have known why Luis put up the fence, but she didn't tell me—just let me get into that awkward scene with Angie.

I thought H was trying to find a better way of leading her own life, not just to break up somebody else's marriage and become dependent on another man. And I thought she liked Gretchen.

That time when H was about fifteen and Mother caught her climbing up the fire-escape ladder to her bedroom window late one night. I wonder why Mother dragged me into it. I was asleep and didn't even know H was out, but I remember Mother opening my bedroom door, and the light from H's room woke me up, and I got up and stood in the doorway in my pajamas and saw H. She was standing in front of her open window and it was raining and her hair was wet, and the curtains were blowing out into the rain. H was wearing red lipstick and crying. She wasn't allowed to wear lipstick yet.

Mother gripped the shoulder of my pajamas. "What do you think of that, Anne? What do you think of your big sister climbing out the window of her own house?"

And I don't remember any more.

I don't believe I've thought about that since it happened, and H has been married so long that I suppose I think of her as always washing diapers in the bathtub or cutting up carrots for soup. I don't even know what she's really like in her ordinary life with Seth, when I'm not here.

July 25
Dear Mother and Father—

Everything is fine here. Harriet has just run off with a bathtub designer . . .

Tall, silent men who dislike women. Cowboys or mathematicians. I can't trust them.

Why does it have to be Bronson? But it's true. H loves him, she says, and her eyes shine. While I was away, they made wonderful plans for the future. I knew she would start describing these plans if I didn't look out, so I walked away into the living room to inspect Mr. Romero's excellent plaster ceiling. (He came after all. I can't believe it! It was nice of H to let him in, with all her other preoccupations. Did she and Bronson plot their wonderful plans while Mr. R was on top of the ladder with his trowel and his hawk, working away and tossing down a few wise Indian sayings every now and then? Or did they wait until he left? I realize now that I don't know my sister at all.)

"Was it Bronson who brought you here that night?" I asked her, sounding as uninterested as I could.

She shook her head impatiently, meaning yes. "We

didn't plan anything. He was on his way to see Seth about that new adobe stabilizer they've been experimenting with, and he saw me running toward him down the road. So he took me here because I asked him to, that's all."

She says that when Bronson came here the other day, he really did hope to persuade her to go back to Seth but that while they were talking, both of them realized, simultaneously, that they had loved each other for years without knowing it. How can I believe a thing like that? And yet when she said it, I believed it. "Do you think Seth really misses anything but my cooking?" she asked me. "He sleeps in the studio. Didn't you know? I thought everybody knew."

(I didn't know.)

"What about Gretchen?" I asked her later.

"Too bad about Gretchen! If she can't get Bronson to stay home with her, is it my fault?" H looked down suddenly at her hands, lying palms up with fingers interlaced, in her lap. "No. I'm sorry about Gretchen. I like her, but I can't see how Bronson could possibly go on living with her. She's so melancholy and slow. Doesn't she make you think of the Little Mermaid? She never fights back."

"But does she know?"

H looked shocked. "No, of course not."

"Then what did she think when Bronson didn't come home that night?"

"He probably told her he was in jail. She's used to it."

I was amazed. "In jail for what?"

"For destroying billboards, of course. He and Kurt go out and chop down the signs along the highway, and sometimes the police catch them and put them in jail for being drunk. Which they often are. It's almost a game." I must have looked as astonished as I felt. "Well, don't you think those billboards are ugly?" She demanded.

"Kurt does this too?"

"Those signs ruin the whole approach to the town. You can hardly see the mountains. Of course Kurt does. It was his idea. Somebody must mind, I suppose, but the police don't seem to. They just take Kurt and Bronson to jail and let them out in the morning. It hasn't happened that often really. Maybe three or four times, but Bronson uses it as an excuse with Gretchen all the time. She believes anything."

"Does Seth go with them?"

"Try and catch Seth doing anything that might possibly be bad for his career." She tried to laugh. "When he gave that picture away—you remember? Bronson told me why. It was to impress Ben Wickersham. I should have realized it at the time. Not that it would have made any difference."

July 26

The more I hear about Seth's defects, the more sympathy I have for him. I begin to see why he spends so much time in his studio.

(I wish I had a studio.)

If I were a real writer, S's work habits would be mine. He simply will not have distractions. This may be harder for a woman. (Yes. I don't know why it is, but something seems to happen to our minds when we reach the age of about seventeen, and we become distractable.) H says that when the children were small, she always woke up immediately at the slightest sound one of them made during the night. But Seth never heard them. The only time he notices them crying, she says, is when the noise keeps him from concentrating on his work. He has probably never even had to consider the question of which was more important, his family or his painting.

S's paintings answer questions posed by other people's paintings, H says. She has been explaining him to me lately, in an attempt to balance her own criticism. He cares about light, shapes, relations between things, spaces. He is impatient with anything human and can't bear to listen to the details of the petty intrigues that interest her. "Seth won't gossip," she says. "Not because he thinks it's wrong. People just don't interest him that much." How different from N, who is fascinated by character differences and is always seeing epiphanies in everyday life. It was something we shared.

Bronson came to see H this afternoon, and they embraced and drowned in each other's eyes. I went on plastering the wall near the window, feeling sure I was doing it wrong and that Bronson would make some comment. I became clumsy then, of course; most of the plaster fell out of my stiff fingers, but I went on working anyway to show them they can't expect me to leave every time he comes. (Though I would like to.)

"Anne doesn't approve of us, do you, Anne?" Bronson said. H was curled on the couch next to him while he stroked her leg with his horrid grouty fingers.

I think I would have been able to guess that Bronson is one of those men who embarrass women by fondling them in front of other people. "What do you expect me to say?" I asked feebly.

H does love him, though. I don't want to know that, but I do. How he feels is another matter. To me, any attitude he adopted would seem like a pose, and so I can't tell. He may be trying to prove he is the only man in town who understands true love, or he may be really caught by her, as so many men were in the past, before Seth.

They are going to live together forever after, and they will move to Santa Fe and Bronson will build a theatre for H to act in. This is what they really believe.

(I think I am jealous. I had forgotten that there was such a thing as romantic love or had thought at least that it had gone out of style, but there it was, like something left over from *A Midsummer Night's Dream.*)

But it bothers me that they are so impractical. Bronson prints his poems beautifully, with spelling errors, and I can't help being afraid that means something. He has elegant cheekbones, H says. Maybe, but she can't spend the rest of her life admiring his cheekbones.

Am I the only person in the world who, reading *Emma,* sympathizes with Jane Fairfax? "So cold, so cautious . . . She was disgustingly, was suspiciously reserved."

"Why did you marry him then?" I asked H dutifully as she was hemming the two halves of the elephant bedspread to make curtains.

"I don't know," she said in a faint, wondering tone. "My fellowship at the Playhouse was about to run out, and suddenly I couldn't see the future anymore. I just didn't feel strong enough to face whatever was going to happen to me. It's very simple, really, if you think of it as a choice between marriage and suicide."

"Was that the choice? Poor Seth."

"Yes, it was! Did I tell you what my landlady said when I moved into my apartment there?" She raised her voice to an anxious whine. "I hope you'll be careful with the gas. The last girl here wasn't careful." Her voice dropped to normal. "That girl wasn't at the Playhouse, though. She worked for an insurance company."

"Had she really killed herself? In your room?"

"I used to think about her quite a lot, trying to picture exactly how she did it. Maybe I wouldn't have gone through with it." She laughed. "It would have been too much for the landlady. So I decided to give my story a happy ending instead of a sad one and I married Seth."

"Marriage isn't an ending. It goes on and on and becomes more complicated all the time."

"Of course, but I didn't think of that then. Did you? Why did you get married?"

Why did I? I wasn't looking for someone to support me, anyway. I had been at least sensible enough to get a degree in Library Science, whether I believe that there is such a thing or not. Getting married seemed the right thing to do at the time, I could have said to H, putting it in a deceptively callous way. Really it was because of N. "Because Nat and I . . . because I cared about Nat," I said finally.

"Cared!"

"Well, loved, then, and it seemed as if we would get along together." I was sounding too unfeeling again, the repulsive Jane Fairfax.

"I don't know why *I* have any right to talk about

love, though," H said. "When I married Seth, I thought it was enough if one of us was in love, and I did admire his work. He certainly had claimed to love me the year before, during my great affair with Axel, when I was starring in all those plays and used to walk right past Seth when he waited for me after rehearsals. Sometimes, after I began to be afraid Axel was about to drop me, I used to let Seth take me out for tea and English muffins."

"So here you are," I said.

"It never occurred to me, never, that Seth only wanted me because he thought he couldn't get me. I didn't even notice how unenthralled he was when I burst into his apartment and announced that I was his at last. So we got married. You're so lucky."

"Why?"

"You and Nat have common interests and the same sense of humor and all that sort of thing. And no grand passion to get disillusioned about. At least, I don't think there was a grand passion, was there?" She looked carefully at me. "But you wouldn't have told me if there was, would you?"

"You and I are different." But I couldn't even explain to her that I don't see the difference as a moral one.

I remember H's wedding very clearly, and it was as elaborate as any stage production she was in. She designed and made her dress herself—mine too—and she looked like a Botticelli nymph, with a strip of lace and a few flowers in her hair. There was recorder music and madrigals, and a friend of Seth's hand-lettered all the invitations. It isn't possible that she got married just because she had lost her job.

Or is that why the wedding had to be beautiful?

But I was there, and I felt that H and S together were perfect; I envied the way they looked at each other.

July 27

All these conversations with me on a ladder and H sitting below are very bad, symbolically. They make me seem to be looking down on her.

I remember one time when she came home after she was married, when Melisande was only a few months old. It was before they moved west, and Seth still had his job at the Playhouse. We all thought of him as a scene designer then, though we knew about his painting. We took it for granted that H would go back to acting as soon as the baby was a little older. I was still in college and vague about the future, and it seemed to me that H had planned her life perfectly, in a way I never could.

Melisande was one of those babies with hair. It was brushed up into a curl that flopped over on top of her head. She hadn't known how to laugh for very long and practiced even when she was lying alone in her crib, chuckling to herself with an expression of pure delight. I remember how impressed I was by the soft, unused soles of her feet. Her ears were a translucent coral color when the sun was behind her, and so flexible that they were sometimes bent forward under the edge of her bonnet for several minutes before anyone noticed and turned them back. (She has quite normal ears now, and calloused feet like anyone else, and she is prudent about smiling.)

Why am I thinking about this now? Because I was

wrong to be envious (we always are), because I didn't know what I was seeing? H says now that the timing of Melisande was a mistake and that she never intended to have more than two children. I have always assumed that H has chosen everything she has ever done. (Partly Mother's fault? "Happy news from Harriet," she wrote to me before Tomas. "Another little Huggins due in January." This when we all knew that Seth wasn't making money and H had been sick for a year after Nora was born. My reaction was anger with H for getting herself in deeper, as it seemed to me deliberately. I was wrong then too.)

There was a meeting of the church playreading group at the parsonage during H's visit. They read *The Madwoman of Chaillot*, and Mother arranged for H to do the ingenue part. Between acts the baby cried, and H brought her down to the living room and began to nurse her before the enthralled eyes of a retired radio actor, seven assorted women, and two young engineers. H was a madonna in her blue blouse with her long dark hair falling over her shoulders to contrast with the baby's blond head, and only a glimpse of white breast showing. "A perfect picture," as one lady whispered to me. I think I was the only one to detect a certain impudence behind H's serenity. The engineers were fascinated, and they sat talking with H long after everyone else had left.

Seth didn't come with her on that visit. She didn't talk about him, but it wasn't long before they left for New Mexico and she must have known they were going. I don't think she was unhappy about it though, not then. She seemed excited about something in the future, and I assumed she was thinking of the Playhouse plans for a touring production of *Winterset* and was looking forward to playing Miriamne. No, she says now, it was only that she liked the idea of being an artist's wife.

July 28

A letter from Francesca Schwartz today, a sympathy note that I don't want to understand. When I saw the envelope in my mailbox, with the neat peace symbol drawn under the American flag stamp, I was reminded of Francesca's arguments with the anti-flag faction of the peace movement, and I was amused and not at all prepared for what was in the letter. She seems to think I have heard from N and know all about what he's doing. After expressing disgust with Nixon and the ABM she goes on, too casually, to mention N and his "friend" who have been attending all the rallies together. (She is not only too casual but too vague. The friend is not named.) "Nobody can understand Nat. We didn't know he had such exotic tastes. [Someone I know?] Anyway, we just want you to know that everybody is on your side. Come back, and we'll have a party and not invite Them."

If it were true, I would have known. N and I have always been honest with each other.

Francesca isn't making it up; no matter what political differences she might have with N, she wouldn't spread rumors she didn't believe were true. She must have misunderstood something that I would see very differently if I were there.

N is not capable of any kind of disloyalty or betrayal, I know. Both of us think (thought?) of marriage as a contract, with trust on both sides. I remember how disapproving he was a few years ago when

Freddie W from Sociology joined a health club with one of the secretaries and was seen riding with her all the time in his sports car. Both of us felt very sorry for Jocelyn W. The same when Dean Q divorced his wife to marry a graduate student.

N couldn't have changed that much, could he?

July 29, 1969

N—

Of course. Someone else is taking care of you. Does she choose the right mysteries from the library for you and remember the first names of departmental wives and tell you what movies to avoid? Or does she only do things like sewing on buttons?

A.

Who empties the pencil sharpener?

(I must not mail this.)

July 29

Tears magnifying everything I see, making the room clearer or more blurred every time I move my head. I turn my face away from H and mention the hay fever season in case she notices. But she has other things to think about.

A character in a novel may be unfaithful in marriage; we expect it, in fact, just as we assume that someone in a murder story will be killed. Our own lives are a different matter. Mary Beth? That's all I can think of. But she is a student, and N would have scruples.

"That wasn't what I meant!" I keep wanting to tell N. I have made a terrible mistake—not just about him but about myself as well, and about my own feelings. I have thought sometimes this summer that perhaps I didn't love N anymore—not as much, anyway, as I ought to love him if I were to go on living with him. And I thought I wouldn't mind unbearably if it ever turned out to be true that he no longer loved me. Wrong every time.

On the last morning before I left, N talked as if he really believed he might follow me here very soon. Perhaps he did believe it. So did I, but it was never possible because by that time he had already found someone else. I should have guessed.

One morning last spring when N had just left, I thought, for work, I went out to the corner to mail a letter and was startled to see him in the public phone booth, the receiver held to his ear and his face against the glass. Our eyes met, and I waved. I assumed there was some unimportant reason for his not calling from home—a sudden recollection as he passed the phone booth or something like that. It didn't occur to me to question him, but as soon as he came in that afternoon, he started to explain. "Our phone is tapped, you know," he said. "Or may be."

I just looked at him. "How do you know?"

"It's easy to tell," he said. "Certain sounds."

I didn't believe it, but I didn't argue. At the time, I placed this incident in the same category as the remark he made when I said I liked a student who came home with him one night to discuss ways of revising the graduate program. "He's all right," N said, then paused. "Unless he's an agent." And then he went on to complain about being infiltrated by the FBI.

But of course the unnecessary explanation about the telephone was only an excuse. He was calling someone and didn't want me to know.

I shouldn't have needed the letter from Francesca. "But I told you that yesterday," N will say (this for about the last year), when I know he hasn't. I was bewildered, wondering after a while whether he might be trying to drive me mad, like poor Ingrid Bergman in *Gaslight*. But his irritation when I didn't remember seemed genuine. Later, when it kept on happening, I should have realized he must be telling these things to someone else and then forgetting afterwards which of us he had told them to.

Not Mary Beth, but someone superior to me in every way. Someone who isn't allergic and never has to remind herself about posture. What I can't stand most is the picture of myself I have now. A pathetic, deluded creature that any husband would want to escape. And I have more sympathy with Gretchen than ever.

July 30

It seems to me that every time I give way to impulse and put myself in a position where I might be vulnerable, I miscalculate. As I did today.

I haven't been able to think of anything but N since that letter came. I carry on a constant internal dialogue with him—demanding explanations or giving them or playing back scenes from the past and reinterpreting them. It isn't healthy. If he were here to provide material from outside—even if what he said could hurt me more than anything I can imagine—at least the whole conversation would be something besides a product of my own mind. When I got the letter, I was so upset that I almost told H, but I prevented myself in time, and she hasn't noticed that anything new is wrong. My eyelids are so thick and pink now that it's hard for me to believe she doesn't suspect, but I am grateful. I don't want H to know the kind of thing about N that I know about Seth—not unless it turns out that neither she nor I will see N again.

But I have been needing to talk to someone, and since N isn't available, I thought this morning, it would have to be Kurt. I owed him an apology anyway. Whatever his motives were for speaking against N, he has turned out to be right. There was a time a few days ago, in fact, when for about half an hour I almost wished his Fourth-of-July plans had worked out. I wouldn't have felt quite so humiliated, I thought. I did see this morning that I would have to explain things to Kurt right away so he wouldn't misinterpret my reason for coming, but I thought I could probably do that. And if I couldn't? The idea of revenge didn't appeal to me, but it is possible I wanted to prove to myself that if N didn't want me, there was someone who did.

H was still sleeping. I left a note for her on the table, picked up the two buckets Kurt had left when he brought the *tierra bayeta*, and set out to find his house. I knew it was somewhere near the Rio Grande gorge, and I drove out of town toward Santa Fe until the gorge appeared on my right, a series of deep reverse curves dwindling into the distance, surrounded by sagebrush and sky. The house was unmistakable—a rough wooden structure with a big, familiar window on the side. I wondered, as I approached it, how Kurt was able to stand living with such an impressive view.

Kurt opened the door as I was getting the buckets out of the car. "Anna." The sun in his eyes was making him frown.

I was so glad to see him that I didn't even use the buckets as an excuse for coming. "Kurt, I was wrong." I think I seized his hands.

He pulled them away, still frowning, and patted my shoulder. "Come in."

I followed him into the house, knowing absolutely that I had been right to come. The floor plan was nearly the same as in my house, I noticed, with a kitchen in front and a living room beyond. I could see a pot of pea soup simmering on the back burner of a wood stove just beyond the partition that walled off part of the other room. Kurt was at least as good a housekeeper as I was, I was thinking. "Oh, Kurt," I said, warm and expanding and just about to cry again but not minding for once, still following him. The big window at the end of the room really was exactly like the window in my house. For some reason I found this very touching. A tear spilled over. Then I saw that there was someone else in the room.

Katrin sat silent in the corner next to the window, radiating peace and complacency. "Oh," I said, and turned my back to the light. "Hello." I could feel myself helplessly shrinking into the mean, shallow person I always appear to be when Katrin is there—the kind of person who uses artificial sweeteners and frets about finger marks on the woodwork.

Katrin just smiled. She wore a long blue skirt and a man's T-shirt with part of the neckline cut out, and her hands lay in her lap pink and inert, as if they were tributes placed there by someone else.

Kurt stood near the doorway, apparently feeling nothing more complex than pleasure at having two women in his house at once.

"I brought your pails back, Kurt," I said. Perhaps

Katrin wouldn't stay long, though she looked very settled. Awkwardly, I turned toward the easel that stood in the center of the room holding a large canvas blocked out in areas of blue, green, and pink. "Oh," I said in surprise, "a landscape!" But then, as Katrin's low chuckle began, I saw that it wasn't.

"What a beautiful compliment," Katrin said in her deep, slow voice, "to be thought of as a soft green meadow, a sunset, part of Nature. I will treasure that thought, Anna."

So that was why Katrin had been sitting so still; she was modeling. The portrait would be more recognizable when it was finished, but it was likely that my first instinct had been right and that Kurt did indeed see Katrin as a landscape. Her figure curved diagonally across the canvas, and her breasts and hips were hills.

"Would you like some tea?" Katrin asked in a tone that seemed to diagnose me as someone in need of a soothing beverage.

"Yes, please." I watched her rise, massive and self-possessed, and fill a red enameled kettle from a jug of water on the kitchen shelf. She seemed to know where everything was kept.

"Do you know what was in Katrin's luggage?" Kurt asked. "A can of Chinese tea, a teapot, a haiku book, two candles, a pack of Tarot cards, and a few clothes for herself and the baby. Was that all, Katrin?"

"The wind chimes." Katrin's mouth curved into her usual small smile. She was watching my face.

"Oh, yes." Kurt looked toward the window. A set of glass chimes hung outside from the branch of a tree, next to a big oval basket suspended from two ropes and presumably containing the baby. "Isn't she wonderful?" he asked.

I took a deep breath and returned Katrin's smile. "No baby food?" I don't even own a haiku book.

Katrin, still smiling, glanced down at her chest. "Nature provided that," she said.

I left as soon as I could. I got into the car and drove to the entrance to the main road and then stopped and put both arms against the steering wheel with my head leaning against them. "Damn," I said, so sincerely that N would have been proud of me. "Damn, damn, *damn.*" The last one was almost a shriek. I stayed that way a minute longer before sitting up straight and starting the car again. Then I found I was laughing. Sorrows come not single spies, but in battalions. It was all too silly. I drove to the laundromat on the other side of town and washed the batch of dirty clothes I had luckily put into the back of the car yesterday along with my empty water bottles. I chatted with the Indian attendant for a while, leafed through three old copies of *Newsweek* (no pictures of N), then filled the bottles and drove home.

H was standing on the ledge of the big window, hanging up the finished curtains. "And how was Kurt?" she called gaily.

I wished I hadn't left the note. "Katrin was there."

"Well, of course. Didn't you know she'd moved in with him? I thought everyone knew."

"I didn't." All these things that everybody is supposed to know.

H sat in the window ledge and leaned back against the curtain and the wall. "She got tired of the commune, and Kurt took pity on her. She may move on somewhere else tomorrow."

I wasn't sure. "They looked terribly domestic."

She laughed. "Oh, they would. That's her specialty. It won't last. No one could count the number of women who've moved in with Kurt." She hugged her knees. "Guess what? I have a date for dinner."

"With Bronson?"

"With Seth." She closed her mouth over a smile. "He came just now and invited me, very formal and serious. He's going to cook it himself."

Seth arrived this evening before H was ready to leave, but he wouldn't come inside to wait, just tramped around the yard looking uncomfortable and holding me to blame for H's behavior. "Cuckold" was the word that popped unfairly into my mind when I saw him stop and adjust his glasses to inspect my flagstones. I tried to think of a female equivalent, but of course there probably wouldn't be one.

H was excited and coquettish when she left. "No," I heard her say in her most thrilling tones as she followed Seth down the path toward the truck, "don't tell me what it is. That's the best part of not being the cook—not knowing what you're going to have for dinner."

It was just a few hours later when she returned, still in a good mood. "Beef Stroganoff. Imagine! And he fed the children ahead of time so we could be alone together, and he put a candle on the table and had wine."

"What did you talk about?"

"Nothing very much. He acted shy, the way he used

to be, and he kept leaping up to get things. You should have seen him bustling around with the pans, using every single one we own and dropping them and making sudden banging noises. He had three different cookbooks open, combining recipes."

"Did he ask you to come back to him?"

"Not really. He was too busy with the cooking. He spent a long time out in the kitchen beating something I thought we must be going to have for dessert, and then he never did serve it." She looked wistful. "I wonder what it was."

"Zabaglione," I guessed. "And it curdled."

"What a shame." She smiled indulgently. "He was terribly sweet; you can't imagine."

"Who, Seth?"

"He wouldn't even let me help with the dishes." H sighed. "Actually, toward the end his attitude began to get on my nerves. At one point he implied that he was just demonstrating the kind of meals I should have been serving him in the past. As if for all those years I had never done anything but open cans of beans. He was trying to show me how easy it is to cook, I suppose. That anyone can do it if he just puts his mind to it, and so why do I complain so much?"

Bronson came for her then and they ran out to his car, their arms around each other's waists.

N was terribly busy last year, and yet he had time to fall in love. That hurts as much as anything else. (The blue lines on this paper are running. Anne Despair.) Because N would insist on its being love and not anything more casual; I know him at least that well.

* * *

I was in bed, writing in this notebook, when H came in, very late, from her evening with the Demon Lover. "I've just remembered something," she said, almost dancing as she crossed the straw mat toward the couch. She stopped and looked at me: "Do you know what Frieda once wrote about Lawrence, when she was describing how neat he was, how he always knew where everything was in relation to everything else? 'He never broke anything,' she wrote. Isn't that beautiful? Before he set a cup down, he always made sure there was a table to set it on. It must have given her such a secure feeling. 'He never broke anything.' Bronson is like that too. Have you ever noticed?"

I couldn't answer. H will believe what she wants to believe.

July 31

"Never broke anything? What can you possibly mean? Don't you remember the tea party that Brett describes, when L picked up the poker and smashed all the china, starting with the cups and saucers and ending with the teapot? All the time, he was railing against Frieda in a thick dialect, saying 'thee' and 'tha.' Brett blamed Frieda for making him behave that way. (See what you made me do?) "

"That was different. It was deliberate. He didn't break things by *mistake;* that's what she means."

"So you see Bronson as Lorenzo, and that's why you love him."

But we didn't say these things. I didn't say anything.

* * *

I still can't like Bronson, but when I see him with H, I can't doubt their feelings. They are aware of each other, almost as if they were the same person, and I am reminded of the way it used to be with N and me. (I concealed this in talking to H a few days ago.) H talks so confidently about the theatre they are going to build together that I can almost believe in it myself. Bronson has already drawn the plans, she says: It's to be a modified Elizabethan style, with the center part open in summer and closed in winter, and Bronson can pay for it through a foundation his family has started. (What H always needed: a man with money.) Such dreams have come true before. Why shouldn't they now? Bronson has built several beautiful houses, including his own; his personality should have nothing to do with this. William Morris was difficult too, I remind myself—used to wrench handles off doors and throw his dinner out the window.

She doesn't mention the children when she talks about the future, but she must expect to take them with her.

The Fiesta begins tomorrow—my arbitrary deadline for making this house possible to live in. And, until a few days ago, for hearing in some way from N. H's problems provide an almost welcome distraction from my own. I bought out-of-town newspapers in Santa Fe again but could find no mention even of the college.

If I had known that N wouldn't follow me here, I wouldn't have come.

5

August 1

The Fiesta Queen ("must be of Spanish-American descent") was crowned this evening in the Plaza. Two young men with refined voices stood in front of me, watching. "Ooh, is that the queen?" "Ooh, isn't she gorgeous." They nudged each other. She was tall, with a space between her front teeth, and was overcome at being chosen. The Plaza was lighted by *luminarios* all along the top edges of the buildings.

Parade tomorrow and parties at night. Everyone is supposed to wear the most Mexican-looking clothes possible.

August 2

It was a lovely Fiesta.

H disappeared in the crowd almost as soon as we got there. Looking for her children, I think. A band was playing on the roof of the police station in the center of the Plaza, with singers occasionally trying to be heard above the other noise. The public address system, of course, was out of order, alternately silent or blurting. Lots of horses, and the street packed with people in costume. Did I see Seth in H's gondolier hat? Or Katrin with a stalk of cotton candy? Even Angie, who has avoided me, smiled and waved today. She was wearing an Anglo sheath with beaded trim and had her hair out of curlers. She and her children were waiting in line near the smallest, most inviting merry-go-round I have ever seen. I didn't see Luis.

While I was in the Plaza late this afternoon, watching children scramble for candy from a smashed *piñata,* I suddenly felt that I needed to be alone to think about what I was going to do next. Everyone from my neighborhood would be in town, I thought. But when I got back to the house, I saw Bronson's car parked in front.

As I opened the screen door, I felt an atmosphere of hysteria in the kitchen that was like thousands of jangling wires crisscrossing the room. "Would you like some tequila?" H asked in a thin, controlled voice. She was sitting up straight in the rocker, not rocking, while Bronson stood behind her with his long hands laid across the back of the chair, smiling in the ironic way I have come to realize is the only way he knows how to smile.

"No, thank you." I saw a bottle and three glasses on the table next to the salt shaker and half a lemon. A still life, unmistakably arranged by H.

"Seth was here," she said, her voice still tight.

"I see." I didn't think they would tell me what had happened. I hoped they wouldn't.

"And now we're going out to your local pub, to celebrate the Fiesta!" H jumped up and ran into the next room, coming back with my hairbrush and the gray-green stole. She unbraided her hair and drew the brush through it a few times, holding her head to one side and letting the hair fan up toward the brush. Then she pulled the stole around her shoulders and beckoned to Bronson. "Come, *amigo.* Let us be 'appy." She ran out the door and Bronson followed, with a last oblique look at me.

I went into the other room to give the air in the kitchen time to stop quivering. It's true what they say about vibrations.

It occurred to me just now, when I had finished writing about the Fiesta and Bronson and H, that it was an opportune time for a bath. I brought the tin washtub into this room, next to the fireplace, then lighted the stove and put two kettles of water on it. It's nearly sunset, and the feeling I have, as it often is at this time of day here, is one of an almost suffocating sense of wonder. I seem to have become more sensitive to beauty in the last few days, as well as to pain. When I went out to the well just now to refill the water pails, the sky was more green than blue, and every plant I could see was edged with yellow light. The two horses in the pasture next door stood like book-ends, head to tail. I carried the pails inside one by one, pausing to watch the gradual changes in the color of the landscape. I can understand why the Indians think of the mountains as sacred.

Problems:
A. House
B. N.
C. Writing. (And the rest of my life.)

A. 1. I have to put in the floor before I finish the walls, as I should have realized before I rushed out and bought those tiles. In order to make a baseboard, I must know where the floor begins. I can't just guess, as it would turn out not to be level.

a. Cover floor with sand.
b. Haul flagstones in and put them in place, adding or subtracting sand to keep level surface.
c. Set stones in cement.
4. Cover with preservative.
e. Wax.

I cannot do all this myself. Mr. Romero? Or would Luis know someone?

2. Walls (mostly done, almost to floor).
 a. Dig damp earth out of baseboard area.
 b. Put tiles in place, set in cement.
 c. Finish plastering walls down to top edge of tiles.
 d. Spray all plastered surfaces with powdered milk solution (use H's vac. cleaner attachment) to keep walls from flaking.
3. Terrace (blocks in place for retaining wall).
 a. Put cement in gaps between blocks.
 b. Cover blocks with mud plaster to match rest of house.
 c. Fill center area with gravel.
 d. Flagstones on top.
 e. Preservative.

Of these things, the terrace is the only one I can possibly expect to finish soon. And I can repaint the door and the outsides of the window frames. Benjamin Moore's Bristol Blue.

The kitchen will have to stay the way it is till next summer. If I can't finish enough of this to rent the house for the winter, I can lock the door and leave the key with the Ortegas.

Because, I see, I must be planning, when the summer is over, to go back to the East, Mass. or N.Y. N? I know now, when it may be too late, that I was expecting all along to be able to go back to him too. Back to him and the apartment and the same life as before but perhaps a little better, as if everything would be waiting there now, exactly as it was when I left. But Francesca's letter showed me that N's life continues to go on, whether I am there or not. I was forgetting that. He may own a shirt that I haven't seen, or he may smoke a new brand of tobacco. I haven't shared any of his experiences for over two months.

I wonder if he would talk to me if I went back, really talk to me. He isn't a monster or an imaginary person; he's Nat. I want to see him and find out what he's thinking.

But I don't want to depend on him anymore, or feel that he depends on me. What I need to do is to make a life for myself, whether N and I are together or apart.

(K? I don't understand, really, how we got into such a mess that night after the picnic or why I should have felt so apologetic. I actually thought I had to make up excuses for refusing to make love. My real reason for refusing, I think now—aside from feelings about N that I had almost forgotten I had—was that I simply didn't want to. Scenes in recent novels by women, taking casual female lust for granted in a way that wishful male writers had been doing for many years before—"Come on, you know it's what you really want"—had made me feel inferior, or abnormal at least, because I couldn't entirely believe in such desires. But now I begin to suspect these authors of lying, to themselves as much as to their readers. So often we feel what we think we are expected to feel; sentimentality finds new disguises all the time.

But "casual" is the wrong word here, and as usual I

am overstating what I am trying to say. It's possible that I would have enjoyed making love with K once we had begun—with him if with no one else I can think of at the moment—but as things were, I really did not feel, in any part of myself, that that was how I wanted to spend the next few hours.)

My writing. I have thought about this ever since I read through my notes a few weeks ago and admitted that they wouldn't make a *Household* novel after all. At the time, I was discouraged and mystified by what seemed to be a loss of ability. Although I had never thought I could be a good writer—had always made a distinction between myself and "real writers"—it seemed that now even my talent for mediocrity had disappeared. It was disheartening.

Since then I have read through the notes again. It is obvious, still, that they will never turn into a story that can be printed on that recycled-looking paper in the back of a women's magazine and receive a successful readership reward score, but why, I am beginning to wonder, should I want to write such a thing anyway? To earn money? Surely, if that's all I want, there must be some more efficient and less degrading way of doing it.

I remember the pep talks Miss Mallard used to give the *Household* survey staff during our lunch hour, about the therapeutic value of our work to the bored housewives of America. She was providing us with motivation, she explained. Most of us, of course, didn't need any motivation beyond the pay checks that were helping to put our husbands through graduate school, but the few who had worked there for very long did seem to feel a need either to justify the magazine or to despise it.

As for me, I believe I have outgrown it.

Look! we have come through.

August 4

When something happens that to me is terrible, it's almost impossible for me to write about it directly. I feel as if my fingers had been scalded, as if picking up a pen and trying to write with it would scrape the skin from my hand and make my arm ache all the way up to the shoulder.

"Look! we have come through." Those were the words that came into my mind that night. (The ghost of Lawrence is hard to fight.) It seemed to me that I was finally beginning to understand what I must do.

I noticed a faint bumping sound coming from the kitchen, and I ran to turn off the stove, where the kettles of water were sending up columns of steam that smelled like wet dust. I ran, not because there was any reason for me to hurry, but because I had energy to use up. When I went to the window to pull the curtains across, I stopped to look at the black shapes of the trees against a sky striped in rose and orange. I had an extraordinary feeling of peace and safety.

In the bath, I sat with my knees drawn up and my head resting on them, looking sideways at the fire and at the shadows on the sand-colored walls. The mood of contentment persisted. Everything I could see—the straw mats and sheepskin rug on the floor, the red kimono thrown over the couch, even the plastering tools and stacks of tiles in the corner—looked beautiful to me. I found myself thinking about a passage I had written last winter, a description of a meeting of the English Wives at which I had noticed that the older group of women and the younger ones were equally terrified of each other, exactly like the members of opposing factions in my father's former church. I had written the description, not because there was any use I thought I could make of it, but because I wasn't able to get it out of my mind. Now I realized that it would fit into an empty space in the book I no longer had to think of as my *Household* novel. I saw it as a book for the first time instead of a shapeless collection of vignettes, and I was excited by the idea of working on it as hard and as well as I could. I could make notes every morning while H slept, and when I went back home at the end of the summer I should be able to start on the first draft. I felt that I had become whole, or seen how I could. Look! we have come through.

I became aware gradually of a buzzing outside, somewhere in the distance. At first I barely heard it above the faint hum and crackle of the fire in my fireplace, but then it grew in volume until I realized it had been going on for some time. It was like the sound of an enormous, faraway beehive, and it was coming from the direction of my open front door. Angry voices all talking at once, about as far away as the river or the road just beyond. As far away as the bar at the corner of my road. I was just beginning to wonder whether I ought to go and find out what was happening when the shots came—one and then two more. They were loud and very near, and their sharp, snapping sound couldn't be mistaken for anything else.

I was certain at once that I knew what had happened. Seth had followed Bronson and H to the bar and killed them both, just like the rattlesnake. I clutched my knees and shivered. I saw a picture, small and clear, of my sister lying crumpled on the floor of the cafe next to Bronson's body. Seth was standing over them looking bewildered, with his shirt untucked and his glasses askew.

The voices stopped and there was silence, as if the shots had temporarily used up the supply of sound waves. Then a woman shrieked "Luis! Luis!" The picture in my mind went blank, there was no way for Luis to fit into it. I stood up and reached for a towel. I was shivering more than before. I picked up my clothes and ran to the door where I could dress quickly while I listened and tried to understand what had happened. There were various shouts now, but I couldn't make out any words. I couldn't even tell what language was being spoken.

A rhythmic groaning began and continued above all the other voice with the regularity of an engine. I put on my moccasins and opened the screen door. I couldn't see anything that looked different from the way it always had. The sky was brilliant with stars, and the only other light came from the headlights of cars parked at the cafe or driving toward it. A clump of trees blocked my view of the cafe itself. The Ortegas' house next door was ominously dark. I began to walk down the path to the road, thinking only *Why Luis?* I didn't know what had happened or what I could do, but I wanted to find my sister.

If it wasn't too late. Luis disapproved of H, and he sometimes did strange, violent things when he had been drinking, but I still couldn't understand why someone had called his name. There were several uncoordinated images in my mind all at once now, as if I were in a television studio watching a show on a monitor. I began to run toward the main road. The confusion of voices was louder, and the groaning continued, accompanied by a woman's high wailing.

As I reached the bridge, I saw someone coming toward me. It was H, her face dim in the starlight. "Harriet! Are you all right?" I ran toward her and grasped her shoulders. I could feel her trembling under the coarse wool of the stole. "What happened?"

She was looking past me and didn't seem to hear. "That idiot! People who go around with guns in their pockets!" She took my hand and tried to pull me back toward the house. "Come on."

I didn't move. "Where's Bronson? Is he hurt?"

"Come on back to the house. Can't you see I can't take any more?" Her eyes were black and wide open. "It's all right," she said as I hesitated. "Come on. We can't do anything."

"Is Seth there?"

"Who?" She stared at me.

"And Luis?" But she was walking toward the house now, sobbing, and I followed her.

August 5

What did Luis have to do with it? The important thing is that Luis had nothing to do with it. It wasn't even the right Luis.

I listened to the sounds from the bar as if they were part of a radio play that was supposed to make sense.

Reality is not arranged like fiction. Chekhov says that if a playwright introduces a pistol in the first act, it has to go off before the end of the play. But in actual life it isn't always the same pistol that goes off.

There are always loose ends, coincidences, and things that can be explained in enough different ways to fit into almost any pattern.

Just a stupid barroom quarrel over an imaginary insult. Poor Mr. Romero. I hadn't known what his first name was.

"Is he going to die?" I asked H.

"Of course he's going to die. What do you think? He was shot three times in the stomach."

Am I planning to use this experience?
Probably
Have I learned anything from it?
Not very much.

August 7

Bronson hasn't been here since the night of the murder, and H doesn't appear to expect him. I'm not sure she's depressed, but she seems subdued, as if her source of energy were gone.

She talked about her children today, in a way that made me sad. She wants so much for them and yet has no real confidence in their future, because of the way (she says) she has wasted her own life:

"Nora has talent, I think. She's a born mimic. You should have seen her do Ophelia's mad scene after we saw *Hamlet* on television at the LeFevre's house last fall. And Melly is so bright. But what good will it do them? Tomas is the only one I have any hope for, and I suppose it should be enough if he uses something he might have inherited from me. Besides the bronchitis, I mean. He has a good sense of pitch; have you noticed?"

"Nobody can use all the talents he has," I said.

"No, of course not, but sometimes I think of intelligence in girls as something that nature just hasn't taken the trouble to eliminate, like nipples on men. The only possible use for it is being able to pass it on to our sons."

And that isn't enough for H. As she says, she should have been a beautiful little fool.

August 8

When H and I were younger, we expected life after we left home to be like a Katherine Mansfield story—blue bowls reflected in polished table tops, all color and texture and sensitivity, and no loud voices. Both of us became careful housekeepers because we thought that by arranging our surroundings, we could control them. Untrue.

There was a note for her in the mailbox this morning, addressed in elegant handwriting that slanted backwards. She read the note when I took it to her and then stared at the wall in front of her for a while. Then she nodded to herself and folded the paper carefully and put it into the pocket of her apron. She didn't say anything.

Later she sat on the retaining wall in front of the house and watched me pulling flagstones into place. "Like a giant jigsaw puzzle, isn't it?" she said. The terrace is almost finished, and I have discovered an unexpected talent for guessing which stone will fit where. A product of years spent packing suitcases, probably. "Bronson sent me a poem." H took the piece of paper from her pocket and handed it to me. Her voice was so soft that I hardly heard her.

I read, in the same odd handwriting I had noticed on the address:

> These are the lives we live and
> these are the lives
> that people have to live

That was all. I supposed, by the unjustified right-hand margin, that it was a poem. "What does he mean by it?" I asked H, who sat with her hands in her lap, staring at a hummingbird poised in the air in front of a hollyhock blossom.

"I don't know. That we have to go back to the way we all were before, I suppose." She smiled painfully. "I thought this might happen."

"No, you didn't! Don't you remember?"

"Yes, I really did. He and Gretchen are very close. They couldn't do without each other."

"Do you think it's because of the murder?" It seemed a reasonable question somehow, if not a logical one.

H looked surprised. "I suppose it is. Because the murder was real, and it showed up everything that wasn't. Our plans couldn't have worked out. I see that now, and so does Bronson, obviously. I could still be an actress again, but I'll have to do it without him. We were just playing."

Seth too? But I didn't say it. I don't know whether H is thinking of going back to him. She probably doesn't know either.

August 9

H got up earlier than usual this morning and began to gather her possessions together. When I saw her making the bed before she had had breakfast, I began to suspect that she was thinking of going home. I was making coffee at the stove when I ventured a cautious question.

"That's right," H said, coming into the kitchen and leaning against the doorway. "I'm going back. After all, I have to think of the baby."

"What baby?" I saw that she was watching me.

"My baby. The one I'm going to have in February. You mean you didn't know?"

Of course I hadn't known! "So that's why you're going back. That's the real reason."

She sat down in the rocker. "I don't know. There isn't any real reason." Harriet Gloom.

"But are you sure? You don't seem pregnant. You've looked so pretty lately, so young."

"That must mean it's a girl. One of my doctors had a theory, something about hormones. I looked ghastly before Tomas—all yellow and bony. Seth said my face was like a skull."

"Nice of him."

"Well, it was true!"

So she must really be planning to go back. I was suddenly enraged with Bronson. Why couldn't he have let her alone if he wasn't going to take care of her? But then I realized that Bronson couldn't be responsible.

"I should have known it wouldn't work out with Bronson and the theatre," H went on, "but somehow it seemed to me that if everything got settled, the baby problem would solve itself."

"You mean you knew about the baby then?"

"Well, I was hoping I was wrong."

"Yes." But I was still dumfounded.

"But really I suppose I knew I wasn't. It didn't seem to matter. I was thinking about myself for a change, and I didn't want to have to consider anyone else."

"Did Bronson know? Or Seth?"

"Of course not," H said. "It wasn't any of their business."

"Oh. And what are you going to do about it now?"

She looked surprised. "What do you mean? What could I do about it?"

"Well, you don't want it, do you?" I could never have imagined myself having such a conversation with anyone, especially H. "If you have another baby, you know you'll be set right back where you were eight years ago except that you'll be eight years older. You were blaming Tomas for preventing you from being in that play before he was born; don't you remember? You can't want to have this baby."

"How would I get out of it?"

"I don't know the laws in this state, but if you can't get an abortion here, you can go with me to a state where the laws are different. I could write to that minister, the one who replaced Father, to find out what to do. He wouldn't tell anyone." I shouldn't have said "abortion," I saw from her expression.

"Don't be silly. We couldn't do anything like that; we couldn't."

"It's a little sister or brother of my children, don't you see?" she said before she left.

"That's sentimental."

"Of course it's sentimental, but I keep imagining its face. I can't help it." She was crying.

I know nothing about H, nothing. "Seth won't miss me. He sleeps in the studio." She didn't mean, evidently, that he always does, though (I insist) any outsider hearing her would have supposed that was what she meant. Maybe it was only for the last week before she left him. Or the last night.

August 17

> Roses are sometimes red.
> Violets are seldom blue.
> Sugar is sweet,
> And you are you.

What I wrote on a valentine I made for N the first year we were married, when we were still doing fool things like making valentines for each other. It was a pretty card, in my best Italic lettering in India ink, with a border of purple violets and red and yellow roses, but I think it may have irritated N by being an example of the literal quality in me that he defines sometimes as flippancy, sometimes as lack of humor, and which already was the thing about me that bothered him most. The card showed that I was aware of this trait myself but perhaps didn't even see it as a defect. He was very quiet after he had opened it.

I was young and didn't know any better.

N's friend is small and quick and self-assured. She laughs a lot and talks easily with men, standing just a little too close to them. I saw her last fall at a political rally just as I see her in my mind now. (She wasn't the one, I suppose, but she might as well be.) She walked in with her head up, surveying the room. She was wearing a full-length red coat over a sleek white shirt and long plaid skirt, and her hair came exactly to her shoulders and turned up in a neat little ledge all the way around. She took off the red coat, tossed it onto a chair, and advanced into the middle of a group of local politicians, all in one gesture. The man who was with her stopped to retrieve her coat and bright silk scarf which had slid to the floor almost as soon as she took them off.

N turned to me, amused. "Did you see that? I wonder how many times he's picked up that coat." But his eyes were shining.

The main thing about her was that she looked like someone who could take care of herself. Whoever started the idea that men are attracted to women who cling?

August 18

N, of course, was right last year when he objected to my spending so much time on the new *Household* novel. I told myself till very recently that it was only because he disapproved of my giving my attention to something he saw as having no social value. This was probably not true. When he said that what I was doing was frivolous, it wasn't because I was writing mere fiction, but because I wasn't writing the best fiction I could. That must have been part of what he meant, but I wouldn't see it. Fooling around, that was all I was doing, just the way H and I used to do at the piano when we could have been practicing.

I used to be annoyed with N sometimes for using me as his conscience, for pretending that I was about to object to something he had said, when it hadn't crossed my mind that there was anything to object to. I didn't see that I was using him in the same way. If there were times last fall when I felt that he saw me as nothing more than a typist *manquée,* isn't it likely that at least part of the scorn I thought I sensed in him was a projection of my own attitude toward myself for writing trash on purpose?

What I write after this may turn out to be trash too, but it won't be on purpose.

August 19

N must be all right and not in any particular trouble, or Francesca would have written about him differently.

The Moral Coalition. The name wasn't N's idea, but after a while he used it without irony. ("I'll be late for supper; there's an MC meeting at five.")

Last spring at the teach-in on the Quadrangle, N standing at the MC booth. A middle-aged man with a Woodrow Wilson mouth and a purple-brown suit stops on the sidewalk and begins to question him in an amiable, hectoring voice. "You people think things are pretty bad here in America, I take it."

"Not entirely. Materially, we're better off than other countries. Morally . . ." N wasn't used to arguing on the subject because we don't know anyone who disagrees with us. I thought it was brave of him to try.

"Ah, morally. I agree with you. Morals are degenerating, aren't they? And just why do you think that is?"

"What I meant was, I can't approve of what we're doing to other countries."

"I see. You don't care what Russia is doing, do you? Or North Vietnam or China? You're only concerned with America."

"I care, of course, but I don't feel responsible in the same way." N lit his pipe.

"So what you're saying is that you don't care about the rest of the world as long as we're all right here in America." The man smiled agreeably. "You don't care about every living thing."

"He didn't say that," I couldn't help putting in, not looking at N.

"I'm only trying to find out your position," the man said. He looked amused, stretching his tight mouth. "I'm not from the FBI or the CIA, you know. I'm just a curious citizen." Suddenly he stared at N's pipe, feigning amazement; smoking was a filthy habit he hadn't heard of. "What's that thing in your mouth?"

I walked away. I couldn't stand to listen to any more.

Too many college teachers now are finding themselves forced by their own consciences into roles for which they aren't trained. It isn't only on our campus, of course, and it certainly isn't only N. Magazines like *The New York Review of Books* and *The New Republic* are filled with articles calling for universities to become either more political or less so. All the visiting scholars who gave lectures on the campus last year seemed to feel called upon to defend themselves for being scholars. Only the most stolid or reactionary or self-confident professors could keep on with their research or insist that students actually do their assignments. N has never doubted (before this last year) the value of his work itself, but he is unsure of his ability to communicate with other people. I think that was why it was so discouraging for him to find that if he talked to his students about literature, he could no longer get through to them. They weren't interested in anything but injustice of all kinds. There was plenty of that, and N could see it too and in fact had been working against it in a small way for a long time. Suddenly his efforts seemed very small indeed. He must have begun to wonder whether it was possible that his work, his life, and nearly everything he valued was based on just nothing at all.

The Moral Coalition meetings were irresistible. They were charged with an energy that seemed almost spiritual, because the causes were unmistakably good and people who had never thought they had anything in common could suddenly agree on who their enemies were. N felt finally that he had found out what he must do with his life—and that what he must do had no connection with Victorian literature.

This explanation is too simple, even if it is partly true. It implies that I understand N.

The Dickens book. N's book, I thought, was fine in its first version, finished three years ago. I think he believed in it then too, although naturally he was growing tired of Dickens by the time the book was done. I typed it for him and checked the quotations, and both of us put it before everything else. We were right to, I still think. It wasn't the kind of joyless, parasitical work college teachers so often turn out. Dickens's stock was a bit low when N chose him as a subject in graduate school. N's dissertation and his book later were both written in an attempt to point out qualities other critics were undervaluing.

But just when a publisher seemed to be about to take it, N lost interest in the original version of the book. I can't help wondering now whether that's my fault. I may have pushed him into writing the kind of book I would have written if I had been an English teacher, not seeing that his interests had changed by then. I suppose that in helping him with it I was like Gretchen setting type for Bronson long after he had stopped wanting to write poems.

Last summer when the Dickens as Social Reformer idea struck N, he was even more excited than he had been when he first began to write. He worked every day and every evening till midnight. We hardly went out at all, because he was so eager to finish his book. (This coincided, luckily, with the reactions to my book and could be used as an excuse for refusing inconvenient invitations.) N's term off would have given him the time he needed, I'm convinced.

But I'm not sure, now, that he'll ever go back to the book. The spectacle of himself merely writing criticism during what he sees as a revolution would shame him, as if he were going down the river on a raft that was approaching a rapids, frantically making notes on little pieces of paper, while all around him people clutched the air and drowned.

Without N, I feel naked or formless. No one else understands my jokes. My Extraordinary Twin is gone, and one whole side of me is covered with new pink skin—not painful still, but sensitive to heat and cold and touch.

August 25

Luis Romero. People have almost forgotten how shocked they were at his death. They enjoy telling each other about it, describing over again where they were when they heard the shots, what they thought, and so on. (I have done this too, though I don't say what I thought had happened.) Everyone was sickened and horrified then, but now it has become just one of the local murders. (There have been at least three others within the last year or so.) When I mention this, H shrugs and tosses her hair away from her face. "Everything happens in the summer here," she says.

Some of the notes I brought with me when I came here were about the incongruity of murder—about the way it can occur in ordinary or beautiful surroundings and about how little difference it makes. Because even now, it seemed to me, after all the assassinations and upheavals of the last few years, most of our lives are still taken up with buying food, cooking, driving cars, working at our jobs. Public men have been killed for private reasons and young soldiers have been killed for public reasons, and yet it doesn't show; the wallpaper in our bedroom at home has the same faint green stripes that it has always had, and the almond tree in the back yard is covered with pink flowers at the beginning of every May. I thought (and I must have known already in some part of my mind that what I was working on would never make the back pages of *Household*) that a church might provide an appropriate setting for a story about this. On the night of the Fiesta, when I was thinking about my book, I saw finally how I ought to write it. I was exhilarated.

Then Mr. Romero was killed, and I wanted to throw away all those notes because they were only words. I was ashamed of them. Even this notebook, which had turned by that time into a journal, disgusted me because of its superficiality and distance from the truth. I hated remembering that I had described the bar on the corner and actually thought of it as a setting for a story. But I didn't throw my notes away, of course, and I have begun to add to them. Words can't be expected to reproduce experience, ever. They can only create something new, and you have to be satisfied with that.

Writing in order to record the facts about an event or situation is quite different from trying to find out the truth about it. When I write about N now, when I am away from him, I find I'm not trying at all to describe him as he has ever really appeared to me; I can't resist, for instance, giving him a mustache instead of sideburns, because of a newspaper picture I saw once of an assistant professor who claimed he was being denied tenure for political reasons.

Suddenly I understand something that has puzzled me since I came: why the painters here, the serious ones, do so few landscapes. It's the same as writing about something personal or violent. The scenery is too overwhelming to be approached directly. The painters use the light and colors, and they wouldn't paint in the same way if the mountains weren't there, but they can't even try to paint what they see.

August 26

Reason for being an artist: a dislike of waste. The putting together of scraps of experience becomes an obligation. The artist is sometimes just a housewife using up the leftovers. *This* fits with *that,* and it would be wrong to let them be thrown out. Especially with all the children starving in Africa.

But this habit of seeing everything as raw material can be a troublesome one. In the days after Francesca's letter came, when I couldn't stop crying, I actually caught myself being interested in what the tears did to my vision, and thinking that I ought to write it down, and feeling at the same time that it was inhuman of me to notice such a detail. My suffering was as genuine and severe as anyone's could be, and yet I couldn't help noticing the magnification. It was extraordinary how clearly I could see each separate grain of sand in the adobe wall across the room, and I wondered if glasses could first have been imagined, before there was any glass, by a near-sighted person looking through tears.

And I disliked myself for thinking of that, and I continued to suffer just the same, with the extra burden of having to record the thought that had come to me.

Writers travel through life like tourists laden with too many cameras. I saw a woman in Italy taking three different pictures of the same hideous cathedral. She couldn't stand far enough away from it to get it all in, she was telling her companion, so she was taking its picture in segments, from the top down. She was distraught until she thought of the idea of the different pictures, and when she had finished she looked satisfied. Until the next cathedral.

I am lucky, I suppose, in having a selective memory and not being obliged to use everything. Poor Thomas Wolfe, with his total recall.

August 29

I went to town this morning, hoping to get groceries, water, and mail without meeting anyone who would make me uncomfortable. This turned out to be impossible. If I had been allowed to choose which person I didn't have to see, it might have been Gretchen, I thought, as I pulled into the gas station and recognized her sitting behind the wheel of the gleaming red Volkswagen parked on the other side of the pumps. Then I remembered to be surprised. I knew quite well that Gretchen didn't drive, and yet there she was, in charge of a little car packed with luggage and children, buying gas as competently as any car-pool mother. "And check the oil, please," I heard her say to the attendant just before she turned her head and saw me.

"But you don't drive!" I said.

"Yes." Gretchen smiled with all her white teeth. Her blond braids were wround around her head. She still wore a dirndl, but she didn't look at all like a waif. "Kurt has at last taught me." She took out her wallet and waved a driver's license. "And now I leave."

From the piles of cartons and suitcases that surrounded the two small children who looked at me with round, crossed eyes, I saw that this wasn't just a trip into town for groceries and gas. "Where?" I asked.

"Sante Fe for the present. After that, perhaps Europe." Gretchen paid the attendant who came to her window. "I shall not return."

Why should Gretchen leave now, when Bronson had just gone back to her? "I'm sorry," I said, and it was meant only as a description of my own feelings about the whole deplorable situation.

Gretchen took it as an apology. "Please do not blame yourself or your sister. It is only, there is all this clutter in our house always, in every way. Nothing is finished, ever, or if it is, everyone outside the family is disappointed. When we finally have electricity after so many years, people come to visit us, and they are sad. 'Oh,' they say, 'but the kerosene lamps were so charming.' They would not have such lamps in their own houses, oh no, with the trouble of filling them and cleaning them, but they depend on us to do it, only so they can know that somewhere there are people still who live in this charming, ideal way."

"Yes, I see." But I still couldn't understand why she should leave now. "But your house is almost done."

"Yes, perhaps. But it is better, I think, if the woman who lives in the house is not the same one who helped to build it." She was actually smiling, in a world-weary European way. "There is more enthusiasm like that, and more respect for Bronson."

"Of course there is, but how unfair."

Gretchen shrugged, with the same thin smile. She could endure any situation, as long as she understood it. "Bronson says I'm bourgeoise. Well, naturally I am."

"Mutti, when are we going?" The little boy in lederhosen and embroidered suspenders began to pound on the back of the seat.

"Hush, Karli. Soon." Gretchen leaned out of the window toward me. "I am tired of living other people's lives for them. Do you see? It is not because of Harriet that I go. Or only partly. I was naturally angry with her before, but poor girl, she is a romantic; still will always believe in the future."

A camping van pulled up behind her and began to honk, and she waved to me and drove into the street, stalling twice, and headed toward Santa Fe.

* * *

I parked the car in the lot just off the Plaza and crossed to the drugstore to buy a newspaper. I buy papers still whenever I'm in town, not because I expect to find news about N or the campus, but because I don't want to become like the people I know who feel so far away from the rest of the country that it's hard for them to care what happens. H, for instance, hates Nixon as much as I do, but her objections to him are mainly aesthetic. "How can I admire a man who turns on the air conditioning just so he can use his fireplace?" she asks. "Or who thinks classical music consists of the 1812 Overture?" Houses are too important in New Mexico too, I have found; people can spend a whole evening talking about nothing but mud.

As I entered the store, I saw Kurt walking toward me. He stopped in front of a display of Indian souvenirs. His hair and beard had been trimmed, I noticed, and he wore a clean white shirt, new sandals, and a turquoise-and-silver belt buckle I hadn't seen before.

"Hello," I said, too softly because I hadn't used my voice much recently. "What are you doing here?" and then I was embarrassed. What business was it of mine where he was?

"Looking for a job." He glanced past me at the door and shifted his feet but then smiled in a friendly way.

"Here?"

"Sure. There's a big demand for pharmacists, you know. I can get temporary work any time I need money, wherever I am." He stared at me. "Didn't you know I was a registered pharmacist?"

I looked up at him standing in front of the shelves of plastic tepees and beaded belts from Hong Kong, and I suddenly had a mental image of him wearing a neat white coat with a mandarin collar and off-center buttons. The dependable neighborhood druggist. I could never have thought of him that way before, but now it seemed right. I doubted that I would ever be able to think of him again as anything else.

We said a few more words to each other, and then Kurt hurried away.

Ony my way home I stopped at H's house and found her singing in the kitchen. The room smelled like ammonia, and the table was piled with cooking utensils and containers of food. H stood on a stool in front of the empty cupboard, holding a roll of shelf paper and a pair of scissors. "Hi. You're just in time to hand me things. I can't stop working now, or I'll never start again. What a great housekeeper Seth turned out to be. Molasses and raw noodles all over the shelves." Her voice was bright and fast, and she worked quickly while she talked. I wondered whether she might be trying to fall off the stool.

"This is the well-known nest-making instinct you see at work," H said. "I get up every morning wanting to tear the house apart and put it back together in some new, improved way. Usually I only get as far as tearing it apart, and then I'm exhausted and start screaming at everybody, so look out."

"I saw Kurt in town," I said. "He was all dressed up."

"His wedding costume, no doubt." She had finished the top shelves and now climbed awkwardly down, as if her proportions had already begun to change.

I noticed that her faded cotton skirt was pinned together at the waist where the button wouldn't reach the hole. "He was applying for a job at the drugstore. He's a pharmacist."

"Yes, of course he is." H lined up cans of soup on the bottom shelf next to the row of cookbooks. "You're going to the wedding, I presume?"

"You mean he's really getting married? To Katrin?"

"Who else? I don't know why you act so surprised. Katrin wants to spend her life having babies, but for some reason she's decided she wants the rest of them to be legitimate, and you know how obliging Kurt is." H had been surprised too, I could see.

"But doesn't he already have a wife somewhere?"

"Possibly. I'm sure he wouldn't think that made any difference. I don't suppose this will last anyway."

"I wonder why he didn't tell me."

"He must have thought you knew. It's this afternoon in the LeFevres' patio. Come with us, and we'll shower them with rice." She smiled maliciously and sat at the table, leaning her forehead on her hand. "I get so tired so suddenly. This really is the most unnatural state to be in. I don't know what Katrin sees in it." She was wearing a necklace that looked as if it were made of sterling silver paper clips. It was rather pretty, in a barbaric way, but it didn't go with the worn, carved-out look her face is beginning to have. She pulled at the necklace suddenly and said, "Don't these look like paper clips to you?"

I couldn't deny it.

"I don't suppose they can be, actually. It was very expensive." She smiled. "It's Seth's coming-home present to me."

It occurred to me that she might not have told Seth yet about the baby. Now that I know, H looks so obviously pregnant that I don't see how anyone else can help knowing. But I didn't ask.

She sat there playing with her necklace. "Do you want to know something? I'm not even any good at having babies. I hate every minute of the whole sordid process, but don't you dare tell anyone I said so. I remember when Tomas was taking so long to be born and the nurses wouldn't pay attention when I complained. They were talking about dates they'd been on the night before, giggling and chattering away to each other in half-Spanish. They must have known I was suffering, but they didn't think it was important. I hate pain and humiliation and doctors rummaging around. Both times when it was a girl I was so angry because I thought this will happen to her too, and it's my fault." She was crying and grinding her fingernails into her palms. "It isn't enough that we have to be pregnant and have the babies; we're supposed to like it, and if we don't, there's something wrong with us." She tried to laugh, looking at me. "If they gave grades in having babies, I'd get a D minus."

I knew better than to recommend an abortion again, but I couldn't think of any other way to help her. I couldn't provide her with a job or a bigger income or a nicer husband. She raised her head from the table then and said miserably, "They tie your hands down. Did you know that?"

"I think," I said, "that you should go to stay with Mother and Father when the baby is due and have it in a hospital in Boston, with a doctor you can explain things to. Take the children with you. There's no point in staying here and being a martyr. You're not Katrin."

H sat up. "Well, it's an idea. The children ought to travel more. And it would be so comforting for me to be with Mother." She looked so bright and hopeful that I had to turn away.

Later, while H and I were fixing lunch for the children, she said calmly and conversationally, smiling a little, "The problem is, you see, that I know exactly what the rest of my life is going to be like, and I'm not sure I can stand it."

August 30

What I saw when I looked at H yesterday was a worn-out woman from one of those documentary photographs taken during the Depression, a sharecropper's wife standing in front of her stove with six or seven undernourished children huddled around her. And my first emotion was not sympathy but unreasonable anger with her for not living up to the ideal picture I used to have of her.

Why have I depended so much on her beauty? I had no right. If I notice that her stomach isn't flat any more, that her shoulders sag or her ribs show at the top of her blouse, why should I blame her? If it turns out that my beautiful sister is no longer beautiful, nothing should be changed. My idea of her is still there; it doesn't matter whether the real H still fits into it, or whether she ever did. All I ever had was my idea of her anyway.

I see H as she was; K sees her as he would like her to be. S doesn't look at her very often, but when he does, he sees only that she hasn't turned into the wife he planned to have.

I can't believe she really thought Bronson could save

her or that he thought he could. I suppose it was just that she needed to see her future differently, and somehow, through him, she was able to do it for a while.

And she needed a man who would look at her. One time this summer I came into the kitchen when she and Seth had been quarreling. S had just walked out of the house, and H stood in the outside doorway with her head thrown back and her hands clutching the edges of her apron. "Seth," she called in a tight, choked voice. "Seth. I. Exist." Then she turned and walked past me into the girls' bedroom, not caring that I had heard.

Kurt came up to me after the ceremony yesterday and took my hands and said, very seriously, "You and I, Anna, will always understand each other." Untrue on both sides, although I knew what he meant. Actually, K and I don't see many things in the same way, or even in ways that are intelligible to each other. He is so complex that I seldom recognize him in the things other people say about him. Or that he says about himself. His mysticism, for instance, is a serious part of him, but I can't take it seriously. (A grown man, burning incense like an adolescent and putting all that effort into conjuring up his father's ghost. Really, now!) Although I still like his paintings, I don't believe I even think he's a very good painter. And he is as much of a gun nut as anyone around here. He has talked sometimes about a group of his friends who are plotting to restore land to the descendants of the original Spanish owners and who have collected a cache of guns almost as big as the Minutemen's. They don't even know how to use all the guns, he boasted. When

I said they sounded crazy, he agreed enthusiastically.

When K told me that he was a pharmacist, I was shocked at the snobbishness of my reaction. My image of him was transformed. Then, "Oh," I said. "Like Keats." It just slipped out. I don't think I was consciously searching for precedents.

He didn't seem much interested in the parallel, "Was he?" (At least he didn't say "Who?") But he had made me seem to be showing off again. I couldn't explain that in the unnatural world I inhabit, everyone knows that Keats started out to be an apothecary. So often when we talk, I say something that to me is almost too obvious to be said, and K reacts as if it were obscure. He scarcely reads at all. He likes the idea of my being a writer but would not dream of reading anything I had written if it were by someone else—would read it only for what it might tell him about me.

If I had married a man like K, we would have been like H and Seth. S worshipped her because she was an actress, then captured her, prevented her from acting, and despised her. (Swann and Odette, Marcel and Albertine. You admire the shape of a woman's nose and then find, when you kiss her, that you must look at her from another angle; the admired shape has gone.)

I asked K why he and Katrin were getting married, and he glanced over at her and gave a sort of shrug. "It's what she wants." (Ungallant, as if it were not what *he* wanted.)

The wedding was better than most. I can imagine the people there being nostalgic about it ten years from now, in spite of all the suppressed emotions that seemed to me to be contained within the small area of the LeFevres' patio. Seth and H stayed close together the whole time and avoided Bronson, who was there with his oldest son (the child of a former marriage, I learned, and therefore left behind by Gretchen. I had had no idea that Bronson had been married before). S and Bronson look through each other now with the same lofty, absent-minded expression I used to see last year on the faces of people who thought I had put them into my book.

No one mentioned Gretchen.

The patio was decorated with asters and pine branches. Most of the artists and writers in town were there, as well as a few businessmen and their wives, some of the commune hippies, and three of K's revolutionary friends. The wedding ceremony was the standard one, with "obey" left in and a real minister from the Methodist chuch. Katrin wore her cut-down T-shirt and long red skirt and bare feet, but there were wreaths of wild flowers in her hair and around her neck.

There was a large pot of chili, and Angie brought tortillas and guacamole. Gallons of homebrew from Bronson. Better than most homebrew I've had here—dark and rather sweet like stout.

Dancing afterwards, with music from accordion and guitar. A clear night, cool, with stars all up and down the sky.

September 3

I have not been sick once this summer, I just realized. Not even after I heard about N.

* * *

Is it possible that I understand at last how little I can do to help my sister? I am Emma, and when Emma interfered in people's lives, she was nearly always wrong. (Her one success, in the case of Mrs. Weston, went to her head and made her think of herself as a born matchmaker.) "People get what they want," N has said when I worried about H in the past, but I still don't think that's true. People get what they fall into. I don't think H would have chosen to have another child, not if all the parts of her nature had confronted the situation at once. I think it is the worst thing that could have happened to her (and to the child), but I think too that she will probably live the rest of her life without telling herself, most of the time, that having the baby was a disaster.

Or she may not manage it after all. When I read a book by Jane Austen, I know there is a limit to what the characters will do to each other. But read any newspaper, and you will be reminded that in actual life we can never know what to expect. Jane Austen's characters didn't keep guns in the spice cupboard.

The air is bright and cool today, with a slight breeze that doesn't belong to summer. When I stood on my terrace this morning and looked up at the mountains, I saw that they were brightened by patches of yellow scattered through the green and purple. The aspens have turned, as H told me they would, all in one night.

And I am homesick. I yearn suddenly for pale, drab colors and frilled white curtains with tie-backs. I spoke of this to H today, but I couldn't express it properly. "If you want white curtains, why don't you get some?" she said practically, and I didn't try to explain.

I couldn't stay here much longer even if I wanted to because there are too many things I have to discuss with N. Aside from the obvious questions, there are all sorts of small, practical matters that worry me. Is our apartment still ours, for instance? And what is to be done with the contents? Wherever I have lived, I have managed to make my surroundings look neat, but only I know always what chaos and postponed decisions the surface tidiness conceals. E.g., that box of unindentified keys in the bottom drawer of our desk. What would N do with those, I wonder? The keys have accumulated since he and I first lived together—keys to trunks, bicycle locks, former apartments—most of them probably obsolete but only probably so and therefore impossible to throw away. Or the photographs I have always meant to put into an album—N's childhood pictures that his mother gave me (the one of N, aged ten months, sitting in a stream in diaper-swollen coveralls and gloating over his first fishing pole; the one of him standing solemn and too tall, saluting, with the other boys in his Cub Scout den, etc.). All our camp and school pictures, the snapshots of H's children, the wedding pictures and the ones we took in Europe. No one else knows their chronological order. If N and I are not to be together in the future, surely he will want some of the pictures, and if I sort them now, they must be put into two stacks instead of one. And there are the old report cards and school papers that neither of us has been able to throw away. (An autobiograhical essay in N's seventh-grade handwriting, beginning, "As the son of a World-Famous Scientist, I . . ." touched me almost to tears when I found it, and made me think unkind thoughts about N's mother.) The other papers shade up so subtly through graduate school that there is always the possibility that something might be retrieved from them for publication.

I want to set to work right away. When I look around at the rough walls, the massive spider-draped beams, the violent light dazzling through the window, I wonder why I am here. Outside, the mountains crouch, threatening and strange under heaped clouds.

September 4

There was an envelope in the mailbox today, addressed in Francesca's large, dashing handwriting:

Come back.

There's a good man who has a chance of getting into Congress next year if we work for him. We can't give up now and leave things to the Yippies and the YAF. Come and help. I swear we won't drag you away from your writing.

They will, of course, but of course I will go.

6

October 11

A long letter from H, with Einstein peering through the postmark. Or is it Susan B. Anthony? A sprig of sage dropped out of the envelope onto my desk. The gossipy, exuberant tone of the letter shocks me:

So sad that your house is empty now, but don't worry about it. Angie guards it with her life. Tout va bien, as that gigolo on Melly's record keeps saying.

Can you imagine Kurt with a mother-in-law? A real one, just like all the stereotypes. She turns out to be a Boston lady in Enna Jettick shoes, someone fairly high up in the League of Women Voters. She came to visit for a whole week, and Kurt had to meet her plane alone in Santa Fe and drive her here, being scolded all the way for Katrin's carelessness in having the baby before the wedding (He was too chivalrous to explain about not being the father.) "Why didn't Kitty think of us?" she kept saying. "She should have thought of us."

About the baby, something very sad. It seems that Katrin, in depending so much on Nature, has been innocently starving him since he was born. The Public Health nurse saw him at a party, was horrified at his size and color, and couldn't believe how old he was. Katrin now buys Pablum and all sorts of supplements to make him grow. She has even lost faith in her own milk and stopped breast-feeding. The tragic thing is that it is probably too late; the nurse isn't sure he'll ever develop properly. We are all so sorry for Katrin that we have forgotten we ever hated her.

Kurt has seen Gretchen, by the way, though no one else has. On the way home from delivering Katrin's mother back to the airport he decided, being friendly Kurt, to locate Gretchen and pay a call. He had found out her address somehow. She was there, he says, but when he rang the bell—the first doorbell he had seen in years—she came to the door in high-heeled shoes, civilian clothes, and a hairdo, looked at him, and said "Yes?" as if he were delivering something she hadn't ordered. She was wearing a girdle, he swears. "A foundation garment?" I asked him, and he nodded. They had a polite conversation, but she didn't ask him in, was late for an appointment with her analyst, she explained. She is said now to have had a breakdown of some sort, though whether the girdle is a sympton of illness or of recovery or whether it is only a symbolic figment of Kurt's imagination, none of us knows.

Gretchen's children have had eye operations, which Bronson would never allow because of all physical defects being psychosomatic. Her father paid, I suppose. Did you know he owns a chain of resort hotels in Austria? Sometimes I think everyone in town has secret financial resources. (Except us.) Kurt says the children look much better. They were peeking at him around Gretchen's skirt.

Bronson and his remaining son are building an addition to the house together and planning to use solar heat. In their spare time they stalk through the canyon with guns.

Something strange—Seth has begun to talk of leaving here! Ben Wickersham is gone but remains impressed by him (thanks partly to Katrin, who is welcome to keep that picture) and writes, mentioning grants and sinecures that might be available in the East. Wish me luck.

Your house is waiting. Come back soon, both of you.

Poor Katrin. We were all thinking of ourselves and forgetting that no one could be the goddess she was trying to be. Even I should have known something was wrong with the baby after what Angie said to me about him. (On the other hand, how could anyone, looking at big, bountiful Katrin, have suspected that she didn't have enough milk for her baby?)

So H was wrong (like me) in thinking she could predict the rest of her life. Maybe she should have guessed that the same pragmatism she hates in S would make him decide, when the time seemed right, to leave New Mexico. What Bronson said to me at the beginning of the summer was true: People don't go there unless they have failed somewhere else. What he didn't say was that they can't stay after they have begun to succeed. Seth never really became part of the town. It should have been obvious that someday he would leave.

Whereas Bronson couldn't bring himself to go even as far away as Santa Fe. (It was his safe, familiar way of life that he went back to—not Gretchen.) He built his house like a fortress, with thick walls to enclose everything he valued. It did no good. And now he keeps on building. "These are the lives that people have to live." It wasn't much of a poem, and he isn't much of a poet, but it stays in my mind.

There was a postscript on H's letter, which I suppose deserves to be recorded. "If my baby is a girl," it said, "her name will be Anne." She may even mean it as an honor.

I have been too cowardly so far to ask anyone where N might be, but he has moved out, leaving spaces I'm not used to yet. (He took the typing table! Also the complete set of Dickens and all his notes, which I thought he had abandoned. What does this mean?) Still, the unaccustomed spaces are gradually being filled in. My Craft House rug lies on the bedroom floor, and Kurt's blue-eyed Harriet beams from the wall above the couch, replacing N's Phiz prints.

An unfortunate thing has begun to happen to my new book since I got back. Aspects of H are creeping into the character—based originally on at least four other people—of the Sunday-school teacher who is on the Pulpit Committee. (Not just aspects—sometimes I see her as H.) And the young minister begins to merge, alas, with Kurt. Another set of people will grow to hate me, I suppose. Not H and K, I hope.

But the book is taking shape. When writing comes easily, it isn't even work, and I feel the way Nora did one day when she heard about prefabricated houses. "But that's cheating," she said, astonished. Usually what to do is so laborious that I am conscious of each brick. I don't think I'll keep this journal up much longer.

October 14

Moratorium tomorrow. "President Nixon yesterday mounted an effort to counter the planned demonstrations against his Vietnam policy, and expressed confidence that the American people would not 'buckle' or 'run away' when it really counts. When asked for his reaction to the campus protests, he concluded in reply: 'under no circumstances will I be affected whatever by it.' "

I have been put in charge of balloons. "Will you leaflet?" Francesca asked me. A verb I have never been comfortable with, any more than with the action itself, but of course I will. One of the things I like least is standing alone in front of a bank and asking strangers to sign a petition. The first time I had to do that sort of thing was during the McCarthy campaign, and Millie had promised to go with me but couldn't because of her children's mumps. I was ashamed of minding but realized that the best way to go through with it was temporarily to become someone besides myself. First I tried being a Jehovah's Witness handing out *Watchtowers,* but that characterization was too foreign to me. Then I remembered H in *Major Barbara,* with her head thrown back and that buoyant smile. So, if I think about it, I was being H being someone else. But it worked, and I was able to show more assurance than most of the people who refused to sign.

I was using H then, as I have so often. Be Harriet, I used to tell myself in unfamiliar situations, because I thought of her as someone who always knew what to do. Though even then I must really have known that it was only my own image of her that I could ever imitate. I have spent my life going from one myth to another. Wanting to believe in people as I see them, not as they are to themselves.

We are all romantics, and no one tells the truth.

October 15

Today was sunny and not very cold. God was on the right side for once. I stood by myself in front of the Village Cleaners and Dyers, wearing a dove pin on my gray R.H. Stearns coat and holding a stack of pamphlets and the strings of fifty balloons marked PEACE. I could see the dry-cleaning people peeking out of the windows at me, shaking their heads. Be Harriet, I caught myself thinking; old habits are hard to break. The balloon strings were knotted and impossible to separate, and the people I was supposed to deliver them to hadn't appeared. Students, professors, children, and women walked past me, nearly filling the street. Balloons in six colors streamed from car windows and the handles of strollers. A hand-lettered sign on the sloping lawn of a Greek Revival house across the street said END THE WAR. "Anne, walk with me." It was Cal, an Emily Dickinson man whose wife and children were liberated from him a few years ago by an astrophysicist. I have always liked him. He held out his arm, but I waved the balloons at him. "Sorry, I have to stay here."

Then I saw Nat striding along with his hands in his pockets. There was no one holding onto his arm and gazing up into his face. His new mustache was so much like the one I had invented for him that I didn't realize it was new until after he had passed me.

I could see myself then, standing on that corner ridiculously holding fifty balloons for the rest of the day, while everyone else marched to the Green for the rally. Why should I insist on being the dependable one, even when no one was depending on me? I stepped off the curb to join the march, but the balloon strings tugged at my hand and got in everyone's way. Be Anne. I let go of the strings, and the balloons rose, all at once, into the sky. They were beautiful.

I can't write about Nat any more because we have to talk to each other instead. It may be, of course, that no matter how much explaining we do, the main product will still be misunderstanding. Or maybe not: loyalty, affection, and grace are qualities that do exist. Sometimes. If it is naive of me to think so, those people who deny that there are such things are just as mistaken. Romanticism can work either way.

I don't know what will happen, but at least I know that I don't know. I believe less and less in endings.